Smoke

Another
Jimmy Carter
Adventure

Smoke
Another Jimmy Carter Adventure

Alexander Cockburn &
James Ridgeway

Times
BOOKS

Published by TIMES BOOKS, a division of Quadrangle/The New York
Times Book Co., Inc., Three Park Avenue, New York, N. Y. 10016.

Published simulanteously in Canada by Fitzhenry & Whiteside, Ltd.,
Toronto.

Library of Congress Cataloging in Publication Data

Cockburn, Alexander.
  Smoke.

  1. Carter, Jimmy, 1924– —Fiction.
  I. Ridgeway, James, 1936– joint author. II. Title.
  PZ4.C6595Sm 1978 [PR6053.0219] 823'.0'14
  ISBN 0–8129–0784–1   78–58159

Manufactured in the United States of America.

Contents

SMOKE

Another
Jimmy Carter
Adventure

Sparrow

November 1, 1980.

The giant military helicopter swooped through the night. Vice-President Walter Mondale sat slumped in the bucket seat behind the pilot. To his rear a group of Mondale's top staff fidgeted nervously as they waited for the red ALERT to flash for landing.

As usual, Mondale's mind was a whirlpool of conflicting emotions: pride battling with fear, all cloaked with his habitual sense of inferiority. He was the man the President had turned to for what he had called "a mission of extraordinary delicacy." So much for David Broder and all the press jackals who said Mondale was finished, "slipping visibly in the President's esteem

. . . shunted callously into a small office suite in the basement of the Executive Office Building."

And yet, and yet . . . Was this a plot to destroy him? It was so hard to read the signals on the President's face. The smile had been as wide as ever. The glint in the chill blue eyes which never failed to pierce through his very marrow, again had made his blood pound with the old familiar desire to please and to be of service to his country.

Mondale stirred at the thought. And Joan . . . how proud she would be at the very thought of him once more the President's "enforcer," as she had once laughingly called him. He had not been able to describe the mission to her in any detail as she prattled on about the exhibition of folk art by retarded Appalachian children, held—courtesy of a grant by Mobil—in Morgantown, West Virginia. But he knew that Joan had sensed from the excitement in his voice that the long months of waiting and of despair were over; that his disastrous speech to the coal miners convention in Pittsburgh was a thing of the past.

. Mondale writhed in the bucket seat at the memory of the eggs and rotten cabbages that had forced him from the podium; the hoots of ridicule from the audience as he had scurried from the hall, half dragged, half carried by a platoon of Secret Service men. And after the mad ride to the airport followed by squads of angry miners, there was the final humiliating memory of looking down from the windows of the Presidential plane at a tarmac covered with miners shaking their fists as Air Force One soared away.

Sparrow

"Sir, Sir, Mr. Vice-President . . ." Mondale shook himself out his reverie and back to the present. The pilot was gesturing down and to the left toward a winking red light.

"There it is. The Salem plant. Five minutes to go."

"All right. Tell the White House that the Sparrow is landing." Sparrow? What would the historians say? Was Sparrow another malign joke by Hamilton Jordan?

Swivelling in his seat he peered back at the men and women staff members crushed together in the aft compartment. Raising his voice to a screech over the roar of the prop blades the Vice-President launched into his pep talk.

"I'm proud to be with you tonight. You have been briefed. You all know the importance of our mission. We are here on the direct orders of our Commander in Chief, and we must not fail him. Within a few minutes we will land and open negotiations with the terrorists. I do not need to tell you that they are now attempting to hold this country—and the policies of our government—to ransom. And they will not stop here. Today, Salem. Tomorrow, Washington. We must negotiate, but not from fear." Mondale was about to launch into a brief prayer, but the pilot broke in once more.

"One minute to go."

He handed Mondale the hand mike. The full awesomeness of what was about to happen gripped Mondale as he cleared his throat and spoke into the mike.

"Sparrow to Eagle's Nest, Sparrow to Eagle's Nest, do you hear me?"

"This is Eagle's Nest." A stir went through the cock-

Smoke

pit as the unmistakable flat tones of the Commander in Chief crackled through the cabin.

"This is Sparrow. We are one minute to touchdown."

"May God be with you. The prayers of Mrs. Eagle and I are with you. We're counting on you, Sparrow. Don't screw up this time."

Mondale braced himself. There was a jolt and the engine hum died away.

Silence amid the darkness. A wave of tremulous excitement rolled through the chopper.

The Sparrow had landed.

Eleven Months and Counting

It was the year's midnight, more or less. The nation, that January dawn in 1980, lay comatose and gloomy in the post-Christmas hangover. Sleet fell, prices rose, and the year ahead seemed pregnant with no great promise.

It was still dark in Washington and even in the White House itself few lights gleamed. In the small room behind the Oval Office there was light, a pool of it revealing a desk piled high with memoranda, briefing papers, polling data, press summaries, decision papers. The man bowed over them, reading with mechanical concentration, looked older than he had done four years before: mouth slacker, lines deeper, amid pervasive droop. Jimmy Carter, embarking on the fourth year of

Smoke

his first term, read steadily and sighed as he did so. It was the worst of times: where were the best?

He started plodding through Stu Eizenstat's background briefing paper on outstanding issues for the campaign year that lay ahead.

Government reorganization; there was little to boast of here. After herculean efforts and a major battle in Congress they had managed to shift the Federal Preparedness Agency from the General Services Administration into a new entity. The angry bureaucrats in the FPA were now filing an environmental impact statement in protest against relocation to a railroad siding in Virginia.

He pressed on, shivering slightly. White House thermostats, symbolically resolute in the face of Arab oil imports now up to 73 percent of national consumption, were turned down to 55 degrees.

A Caddell polling brief: the data showed that 67 percent of the American people were prepared to vote to abolish federal income tax. All over the country politicians were running on the issue. The U.S. was increasingly polarized on the issue of nuclear power. On the matter of nuclear war, fifty-six percent favored a preemptive strike against the Soviet Union and 46 percent believed that the United States could survive and emerge victorious in such a thermonuclear exchange.

There was tax reform: the memoranda were judicious but depressing. The tax revolt was still in full swing. Twenty-three states had now placed curbs on property taxes. Schools, hospitals, libraries, fire stations, and public services of all sorts had failed on the local level. Gradually the state and federal organizations funding them had come in to restore the services, with money raised through sales taxes. The right wing, leader of the attack on property taxes, was now claiming the central government had taken over the country.

Carter's eye wandered sideways to Presidential Review Memorandum No. 128. It concerned itself with the future energy policy of the United States. A young schemer in the National Security Council was arguing briskly that U.S. energy needs could be solved by what he called grandly "a Continental Plan." Under this Plan all legal barriers to aliens coming to the U.S. from Mexico and Canada would be abandoned. The *quid pro quo* for the U.S. would be cheap imports of Mexican oil and Canadian coal, gas, and other fuels.

The President read on curiously. The young schemer concluded his suggestions with a laconic addendum on the side-benefits of suspension of border controls with Mexico. "A major contribution to the battle against inflation would be the influx of cheap labor to reduce wage levels. And, since these alien workers are eager to work hard—harder than our own labor force—productivity would be raised.

"Moreover the Plan would have other salutary effects. It could be used to bolster the family. The influx of Mexicans would help to push our women out of the work force, through downward pressure on wages, and thus would make it possible for American women once more to return home and have children. The alarming decline in the birth rate would thereby be arrested."

Smoke

In twenty years, PRM 128 concluded, given present trends in white middle class birth rates, states such as California and cities such as New York would be—to all intents and purposes—"third world entities."

The President brooded, mentally framing a speech. "Our ethnic integrity is being threatened"—too controversial. "We need more white children"—too crude. "The burden of producing children must no longer be left to the more underprivileged sectors of our society." This might work.

He rose behind his desk and tried it out: "The . . . ah . . . . burden to our poor people of raising children needed for the preservation of our country's greatness must be . . . ah . . . lightened."

"What must be lightened, Mr. President?" With a start Carter found himself staring into the eager eyes of Zbigniev Brzezinski, director of the National Security Council.

"Tell me, Zbig. What do you think the major crises confronting our nation are today?"

"Soviet aggression, Cuba, and the perceived threat of the SS-25," Brzezinski rapped back automatically.

"And?"

"The failure of the advanced industrial nations to come to a common agreement on tariffs?" Brzezinski looked at him uncertainly.

"And?"

"The French? The Chinese? I don't know. Has something happened during the night?"

The President shrugged. "No, nothing at least that

they've bothered to tell me about. I was just thinking about women."

With a furtive glance at his Commander in Chief Brzezinski launched into his daily intelligence briefing, a machine-gun recitation of the world's ills. The Soviet Union was militarizing the South Pole. He recommended an expeditionary force of Argentinians without delay, with open U.S. funding. President Giscard d'Estaing had switched analysts and had a new girl friend. The Israeli government was not being helpful in the matter of its new settlements in Southern Turkey. The Chinese were signing a treaty of friendship and mutual security with the West Germans.

The President grew weary. He fell back on a time-honored ruse to rid himself of the loquacious and conceited Pole. He raised the volume control beneath his desk and Shostakovitch boomed from the concealed speakers. Russian music. With an expression of distaste Zbig concluded a pessimistic survey on prospects in the new session of the Law of the Sea Conference and left the room.

The minutes clicked by like hours: meetings and then more meetings; with representatives of the Business Round Table, with the grain traders, with some Georgia school children, with the new ambassador from Uganda. A peanut butter and jelly sandwich and it was time for his cabinet meeting.

All were present, except for Vice-President Mondale, away on a good will mission to Equatorial Guinea.

Smoke

Carter addressed them briefly.

"Ladies and gentlemen, I am proud of you all. You are superb appointments, probably the most highly qualified group of government officials ever to have assembled in one room. And therefore you probably know what I am going to ask of you this morning, and will continue to ask in the weeks and months ahead."

He paused and smiled around the room.

"I want to hear from each of you what you have done and are doing to contribute to my re-election efforts."

Up shot the hand of the Secretary of Transportation. "Over at my department, Mr. President, we have taken the lead in your re-election campaign. I am proud to report that more than $2 million has already been committed by our great trucking industry."

"How exactly did you manage that?" asked Juanita Kreps nastily.

"By the spring of this year Amtrak passenger service and, more importantly, Conrail freight service will be severely curtailed."

Carter turned to the Secretary of Agriculture. "Bob, what about the farmers?"

"Mr. President, I have encouraging news. The Indian subcontinent is still enduring one of the worst periods of drought and famine in the twentieth century. And as you know, the Soviet Union has been similarly afflicted. Our grain sales are at record levels. For the first time in more than a year it is entirely secure for you to visit Iowa, Kansas, or Nebraska."

"Wonderful, Bob. We should, however, indulge in a moment's prayer for the millions of starving people for

whom American aid has probably arrived too late."
They prayed briefly.
Carter turned, somewhat deferentially, to Secretary of Defense Harold Brown.
"What has the Pentagon in store for us, Harold?"
Brown spoke briskly in an arrogant manner.
"Mr. President, I would not wish it to be thought that our national security could be compromised by a matter so peripheral as the democratic process. Nonetheless I have done my duty."
Brown cleared his throat. "I am pleased to announce that after discussion with Mr. Patrick Caddell the Defense Department has initiated major procurement programs in all localities designated by Mr. Caddell as undecided in the forthcoming electoral contests. The shelter building program is now estimated as providing 2 million jobs. Our overall defense posture is one of increased preparedness, in light of the expanded Soviet threat. This preparedness is being indicated to the media in daily briefings."
The discussion wore on. They were deep in contemplation of a complex housing guarantee program for the inner city when the President edged back to a theme that had been concerning him all day.
"Our population growth is sinking below zero. In the not too distant future the ethnic integrity of our country will be gravely compromised."
Silence. Carter turned to the Secretary of Health, Education, and Welfare. "Mr. Califano, I would like to have a memorandum from your department with proposals to counter this trend by the end of the week."

After the meeting an austere figure entered the Oval Office abruptly. The President was speaking agreeably into the telephone. "Alright David. I'll check with Bill Miller about your problem and I'll get back to you later. In principle I see no objection to Chase buying this particular island."

He put down the phone and looked up at the flushed countenance of James Schlesinger, his Secretary of Energy.

"Jim?"

Schlesinger spoke urgently. "Mr. President, one basic fact was entirely omitted from consideration in your cabinet meeting. The most contentious opposition to your re-election—largely from within the ranks of your own party—are the anti-nuclear demonstrators. Do you realize how extensive this movement is? There are now 5000 such groups in this country. Already there have been 23 major demonstrations this year. Everywhere I go I experience the rampages of these so-called practitioners of non-violence."

"I know, Jim. It's getting worse all the time. But politically the situation is very delicate. This movement, especially after the accident in West Germany, commands a wide measure of support."

"May I suggest that to start with we set up a special task force."

"Another one?"

"Yes. I propose that I chair an inter-agency group to examine our options. Establish contingency plans to counter further demonstrations and active sabotage:

proposals to deflect the imminent bankruptcy of two of the largest nuclear plant manufacturers in this country."

Carter nodded, his mind already returning to the problem of ethnic integrity. "Get onto it right away."

Five minutes later Ham Jordan poked his head round the door. "Jimmy, I was just thinking. If Bert managed to sell American industry to the Russians, they'd never want to attack their own property, would they?"

Eleven months to go.

Love and Poison

Julie Lindner lay on her back on the rich New Jersey earth, staring up into the blue sky across which scudded white, plump cushions of cloud from the industrial heartlands of America, swollen with sulphuric acid, pregnant with carcinogens. Nature's little hearses.

Near her Jack Dunn dug his fingers into the soil, fecund with endrin, aldrin, dieldrin, phosphates from the far-away deserts of Mauritania. He sniffed the rich tang of chemicals and quickened at the thought of the hidden elixirs mixed by the hand of man in this good earth—cadmium, lead, arsenic; tilth and foison from the sludge borne down by the Delaware River.

Julie shifted her gaze from the clouds to the great dome of the sky itself, a kaleidoscope of purposeful movement that tender, warm spring day. Nearest the surface of mother earth herself a light biplane dipped and plunged as it sprayed paraquat over a field of weeds. Thirty thousand feet up a wide-bodied passenger jet hovered almost motionless. Was that tiny speck falling down and away from the elegant silver pencil a hijacker, an engine? Julie did not know. And above the passenger jet, twin fighters on a test flight from Grumman played tag across the sky. Off in the distance the thin needle of the Concorde shimmered.

"It's great to be alive," she said contentedly.

"Sure is," said Jack.

Oh, and far down inside her the deeps parted and rolled asunder, in long, far-travelling billows, and ever, at the quick of her, the depths parted and rolled asunder . . . As the plunger went deeper and deeper, touching lower, she was deeper and deeper and deeper disclosed, and heavier the billows of her rolled away to some shore, uncovering her . . . the quick of all her plasm was touched . . . the consummation was upon her . . .

"Are you going to hear Nader talk at Princeton?"

Julie's fantasy came to an abrupt halt, as Jack repeated the question.

"I suppose so." She tried to resume her reverie, which had been producing some satisfactory sensations. Jack was inexorable, immune to the rites of spring.

"It's meant to be a debate. Who do you think they'll have on the other side?"

"I don't know. Edward Teller probably." She rolled over and looked at Jack.

Love and Poison

"To be frank, I'm not sure I do want to go to another debate about nuclear power, pro and con. I know the arguments, you know the arguments. My mind's closed. I'm against it."

"I know what you mean." Jack began to declaim at the biplane. "The fact of the matter is, ladies and gentlemen, that less people have been killed in nuclear accidents in the last ten years than have been slaughtered this year on the New Jersey turnpike by the most potent instrument of destruction in the United States, the automobile. While I yield to none in my esteem for solar power I would not be honest if I did not tell you that by the year 2050 the sun will be furnishing precisely one-sixtieth, *one-sixtieth* of our nation's energy needs. Blah, blah, blah."

With a last energetic drizzle of paraquat the biplane retired in search of fresh weeds to conquer.

In the arsenal of democracy, as perceived by the President and his colleagues, Jack was a disaffected element. At 27, he was a skilled mechanic for the local Honda distributor with a BS degree in animal husbandry from Penn State. His mother had died some five years before from simple attrition of all working parts —a natural death. His father had passed on shortly thereafter, felled by a carcinoma in his stomach after many years of devoted toil in an asbestos factory.

Dimly rooted in Jack's mind were the marches of the late sixties. He had read about World War II and knew that Jack Kennedy had been assassinated by a conspiracy of Texan oilmen. When asked by an itinerant pollster for his leading concerns, Jack had replied nastily,

Smoke

"I have three interests in the following order. One, riding my bike. Two, smoking dope. Three, fucking my girl."

This was not quite true. Jack, an ardent vegetarian and admirer of the works of nature, was against pollution in all forms, starting with Tom Snyder, heading on through pesticides, and finishing with microwaves, low-level radiation, and nuclear energy, military or civil. He lived in a trailer equipped with a cedar-wood hot tub and presently enjoyed Julie—whom he had met at an anti-nuclear teach-in—even more than his bike.

After shaking his fist at the biplane he resumed his declamation. "You ask me, ladies and gentlemen, about the so-called problem of nuclear waste. Only a society as self-indulgent as ours could become so obsessed about this matter. If we cannot bury it in the ground—which we can—and if we cannot sink it in the sea—which we can—why then we can place it on a space ship and fire it at the moon. And do you know what will happen, ladies and gentlemen? Ralph Nader will file an environmental impact statement on behalf of the man in the moon!"

He paused for breath and looked at Julie, a comely and indeed most desirable warrior in the fight against nuclear power, which for her had begun at home. Her father had been a utility company executive in charge of nuclear plant construction. Crippled in the collapse of part of a new plant, with the loss of both his legs, Mr. Lindner had enjoyed the unpleasant experience of receiving a small gold watch and the brisk farewell of a company for which he worked for 25 years. Now he sat

Love and Poison

in a wheelchair in front of the cash register of the small
diner run by Julie's mother on the Camden truck route.
Julie was their joy and, at 30, still their hope. Scholar-
ships; graduate of Douglass College, N.J., law degree
with highest honors from Yale; offers from New York
law firms including Simpson Thacher and Cravath,
Swaine and Moore. These offers had been spurned. Instead Julie had busied herself with the public interest
movement. She had worked on Ralph Nader's Dupont
Project, conducted investigations into byssinosis for the
Carolina Brown Lung Association and had represented
the anti-nuclear movement in Pennsylvania in its
efforts to stop construction of a nuclear-powered energy park in the central part of the state.

   She became militant. Tiring of the conventional legal
approaches she had turned to politics and worked on
major campaigns in both New Jersey and Pennsylvania.
Her passionate affair with a populist running a doomed
bid to become Pennsylvania attorney general had
turned her to radical paths of thought. She was active
in local anti-nuclear politics now, and represented several different groups before state regulatory commis-
sions and in Washington at Department of Energy
hearings. In any given week she was back and forth in
court appearances at Trenton, Harrisburg, and the
Federal District Court in Washington.

   She opened her eyes and gazed at Jack who had now
switched sides in the debate and was ranting fiercely,
stabbing the air in the general direction of New Jersey's
finest, the Salem nuclear power complex, just over the
horizon to the south. He spoke of carcinogens, which

she had heard about before. He spoke about the expense, danger, waste, and downright awfulness of nuclear power, which she had heard about before. He expanded his theme and recalled that a million times the amount of nuclear power dropped on Hiroshima was now in the hands of the military men, which she had heard about before.

He was right and she was right and no doubt millions of their co-citizens and fellow thinkers were right too. So where did that get them?

"What we ought to do," Jack was concluding, "is to take over that goddam plant and shut it down."

"Before you do that," Julie said as she produced a file from her bag, "why don't you look at this?"

Jack took the thick, xeroxed, unmistakably official government document and observed the paroxysm of federal security instructions stamped on the cover. TOP SECRET—EYES ONLY.

"What's this?"

"I have a friend in Washington," Julie said discreetly. "This was done in the last two months. It's being reviewed now. I thought we might get some ideas out of it."

Julie's blonde head resting comfortably in his lap, Jack started to read.

How to Bring the Nation to Its Knees

MEMORANDUM FOR THE PRESIDENT
ON FUEL SYSTEMS VULNERABILITY
WITHIN THE CONTINENTAL UNITED STATES

Prepared by the Inter-Departmental Task Force on Energy

In view of the worldwide concern over terrorism, the President has created an Inter-Departmental Task Force on Energy, lodged in the Energy Department to co-ordinate security measures and form contingency plans. This report addresses itself to potential internal threats to the nation's energy security. External threats—

to tanker routes, strategic commodities, etc.
—will be dealt with in a separate memorandum.

Summary
   While the United States is abundantly
endowed with reserves of major mineral fuels
(oil, natural gas, coal, shales) the supply of
these fuels is vulnerable to terrorist attack
and interdiction. A survey by this office
makes clear that population centers could be
severed from fuel supplies with considerable
ease. There is presently no federal
contingency plan to deal with this threat.

   Pipeline Interdiction
   Though it is popularly assumed that
terrorists and saboteurs would direct their
attention to oil refineries, electric
generating equipment, or nuclear power
plants, in fact it is beyond doubt that the
most vulnerable part of the energy supply
system within the continental United States
are the transmission facilities for oil,
natural gas, and electricity.
   Natural gas and oil are generally
transported within the United States through
pipelines. Indeed, the North American
continent is covered with thousands of miles
of interconnected pipelines. There are nearly
250,000 miles of oil pipeline alone—a
cumulative total in excess of all the railroad
track in the U.S. Pipelines not only transport
liquids and gases, but also solids and
slurries.
   To give a preliminary idea of the

vulnerability of the pipelines, the compilers
of this report can do no better than to quote
from *Vulnerability of Total Petroleum
Systems,* by Stephens, M.M., May 1973, U.S.
Department of the Interior, Office of Oil and
Gas (unclassified):

> A gas pipeline can be bombed over a considerable
> length by a single charge. It will blow up by it-
> self if a break allows air into the line. An air-
> gas mixture in a pipeline, under right condi-
> tions, can explode and detonate over miles of
> terrain, through cities and industrial centers.
> Damage to a sizable line would be measured in the
> millions of dollars and could cause complete de-
> struction of segments of the line. It is seldom
> that just a small section of the line is de-
> stroyed. The writer observed an 8-inch spiral
> weld line that unwound and came out of its ditch
> for a distance of eight miles. A larger line would
> result in a worse situation.

Natural Gas Pipelines: There are 65 gas interstate pipelines operating in interstate commerce. Of these, 24 carry 97 percent of all natural gas, which represents one-third of the
nation's energy supplies. Out of these 24,
there are 4 lines of crucial importance. They
are as follows:
* El Paso Natural Gas, whose lines extend from
Texas to California, making it a major supplier
to Los Angeles, which is the largest single market in the country.
* Tenneco—a conglomerate which owns Tennessee
Gas Transmission Co.—operates Tennessee Gas

Pipeline extending from producing fields in Texas and Louisiana to the populous east coast, including New York City and Boston.
 * Two companies, Texas Eastern and Transcontinental, operate pipelines from the Gulf of Mexico to the mid-Atlantic region (including the Washington metropolitan area) and on into New York City. Texas Eastern, through its minority holding in the Algonquin pipeline system, may be considered a major supplier of gas into New England, where Algonquin operates.

Interdiction Prospects
   Interdiction of the pipeline system would be a simple task for any terrorist group. It can safely be said that any saboteur furnished with the most rudimentary equipment (a shovel, a bulldozer) could disrupt the integrity of a pipeline.
 * Natural gas pipelines are concentrated in a relatively narrow right of way, less than 150 feet in width. Maps of pipelines, though not designating specific placement, are available in the Department of Energy and are routinely published in industry journals. State laws require that pipeline crossings be marked when they go under a road or river.
 * In the case of natural gas, compressor stations along the pipeline system are especially vulnerable. If only one station is damaged, then adjacent stations may supply enough pressure. But if several stations are damaged along a line, it may take a considerable time to repair the transmission system. Furthermore, spare

parts for pipelines do not exist in any quantity and must be made specially. This could lead to further delays in recovery.

* Imperiling gas (and indeed oil) pipelines and compressor stations is the fact that only a very few people operate these facilities. Many stations are controlled automatically and are totally unmanned. Repair crews are lightly manned. Since supervision of the system depends largely on computers and microwave sets, controlled by a handful of technical personnel, it is easy to envisage a situation in which the physical attrition of such highly trained personnel could create significant problems, delaying repair.

* Gas is delivered to the "city gate" of a community, where it passes through a set of regulated meters and odorization equipment before reaching the ultimate consumer. In the older cities of the United States, particularly those on the eastern seaboard, the gas piping infrastructure within the city is antiquated. Many of the fires in a city such as Baltimore in recent years have been traced to such antiquated piping, which can break or leak. Given these circumstances, if a group of saboteurs were to substantially increase the gas pressure on lines serving residences or public buildings, these lines and/or appliances could rupture and the escaping gas could cause numerous fires and explosions.

The following are two scenarios, to demonstrate gas pipeline vulnerability:

Scenario No. 1
A small group of terrorists seek to interdict the California natural gas pipeline system, shutting off Los Angeles from gas supply. Gas in California is provided from three major sources. The bulk comes from the Southwest, via the El Paso system, and goes directly to the Los Angeles market. A smaller, but nonetheless important pipeline system brings gas from Canada down through Washington and Oregon into the San Francisco market. A third, much less important, supply line collects gas produced in the southern sector of the Central Valley and carries it northward along the valley floor to industries clustered outside San Francisco.

Interdiction of Los Angeles would require two simple steps. First: obtain a general map of the El Paso system from the Department of Energy, American Petroleum Institute, or an industry journal, and precisely locate the target. Second: select a point along the line, preferably in the desert, and sabotage by bulldozer, explosive charge, etc. The result would be a severe strain on the supply system in Los Angeles, probably leading to a shutdown of industry and a gas black-out for consumers.

Repair of the line would take several days and, of course, if the terrorists were prudently determined, they would have taken the precaution of blowing up the pipeline in several different places.

Scenario No. 2.
A slightly more ambitious plan, requiring a larger measure of organization and financing,

would lead to interdiction of gas supplies to
the entire state. Two strikes would be re-
quired. One in the desert in the south, and another in the forests of northern California.
Probably such a plan would require use of aircraft to ensure timely departure from the
sites. The result would be total interdiction
of gas supplies for the largest and most populous state in the union; the closing of major industry including oil refineries and electric
utilities. It should be remembered that because of the interconnection of different fuel
systems the severing of a natural gas pipeline
over any period of time will place critical
pressure on the electric utility system. In all
probability such pressure would cause escalat-
ing failure of the electrical system, with obvious consequences for industrial and public
chaos.

Oil Pipelines: The problems presented with oil
pipelines are somewhat less alarming than with
natural gas. Natural gas is intensely volatile. Oil, unlike gas, is routinely transported by means other than pipeline, i.e.,
truck and ship. (The Northeast, for example, is
dependent on oil imported by tanker.)
Oil pipelines are interlinked to a degree that
reduces their vulnerability.
As with natural gas, oil pipelines are most
vulnerable at unguarded and unmanned pumping
stations. These pipelines systems, it should
be emphasized, are all too often run from single
control stations. Stephens, in his *Vulnerability* study, notes:

One small room, in a large southern city, houses the complete pipeline control system and controls oil movement over several states. Valves can be closed or opened, pumps can be started or stopped, even though they are miles away. Forced entry to the computerized center, the cutting of wires, the mutilation of the printed circuit boards, the burning out of low voltage circuits by tying them to the house current, the careless use of a strong magnet, could suddenly put the entire system back on hand operation. Each control valve, of many hundreds, would have to be visited, but now only a few men are available to run the system. There are no repair crews except for contract crews in most cases.

A final point: where oil and gas are the source fuels for electric utility operation, attacks on a pipeline would seriously endanger the production of electricity whose vulnerability will now be considered.

Electricity Interdiction
   The electrical supply system of the United States is especially vulnerable to attack by small groups of saboteurs or terrorists. During the anti-Vietnam war movement of the late 1960s there were several different attacks on transmission facilities in the Northwest and in California. Fortunately the saboteurs struck at that part of the system most easily repaired: transmission wires or supports that

could readily be replaced or bypassed with jury-rigged systems. If, however, they had taken their cue from various natural disasters, large parts of the nation could have been without electricity for days, weeks, or even months.

The blackout in New York City during July 13, 1977, was initially blamed on a lightning strike to transmission lines 50 miles north of the city. However, the blackout was assured by the fact that a major interconnecting line from Manhattan to Jersey City (the Hudson-Farragut tie) was out of commission, thus leaving the Con Ed system fatally weakened. Suffice it to say that the severing of one line in the Con Ed system, and the damage of one generating station, could easily result in the denial of electricity to a metropolitan area with 16 million people, and if properly timed could cause a rolling blackout on into New England.

An attack on electricity production systems in one of the older cities along the eastern seaboard, where wiring, switching terminals, and other equipment are underground, would require complex and time-consuming efforts for repair.

The reason for what the Task Force considers to be the complete vulnerability of east coast electric systems is the failure of the electric utilities to agree to develop a common interconnecting grid that is in turn locked into other national grid patterns.

It is true that there is a grid of sorts in the Northeast. The New England power pool is meant

Smoke

to be connected to the New York power pool, which itself seeks to relate the upstate systems to the New York metropolitan area. The New York systems are theoretically connected to the so-called PJM (Pennsylvania, New Jersey, Maryland) pool to the south. (In fact, as the 1977 New York blackout demonstrated, this intertie is insufficient to support the northern systems.)

The PJM interconnection, accomplished through a computer station at Valley Forge, Pennsylvania, is the single most important junction in the eastern grid. Flowing into the PJM switching stations are massive amounts of electricity from south and west, but because of the incapacity of the eastern utility systems and the poor interconnection, these blocks of electricity are often unusable. This is especially true at peak seasons of the year.

It is the judgment of the Task Force that the eastern seaboard is vulnerable to attack and grave destruction at every point from Washington to the Canadian border.

Electric System Interdiction

Scenario No. 3.
A terrorist strike at Con Ed underground transmission supply systems, severing wires, damaging switches, etc., probably—though not certainly—would lead to collapse of that system, turning off electricity to 16 million people. Damage to a generating plant would severely damage the system, leading to its collapse.

Scenario No. 4 .

A group of terrorists attack the PJM computer station at Valley Forge, gain entrance, take over computers, and signal member plants to shut down. Failure of manual operators to detect computer signals and intervene with sufficient speed will result in a rolling blackout of the Washington, Baltimore, and Philadelphia areas, with a strong possibility of rolling blackouts northward into the weakened Con Ed system.

Communications Vulnerability

Since computers play such an important role in the management of energy fuel transmission systems it is important to realize that computer control centers are especially vulnerable. The possibility of forced entry by a group of competent saboteurs is an obvious danger, and one where protective measures can be taken.

But there are far more subtle forms of sabotage. For example, a saboteur may pose as an employee, gain entrance to the computer operations, and man a position for months or years. Through artifice he can wreck the computer and bring down the energy system. He may adopt any one of a number of tried techniques. The "Trojan Horse" trick is one example. It involves the saboteur twisting the program in such a way that all control is given to one terminal of which he has command. The "time-bomb" trick involves the saboteur programming some seemingly harmless word, such as the name of the saboteur, in such a way that once his name is printed out, all the computer tapes are erased. It is, of course, known that a computer can be severely damaged through the use of magnets or by the simple pouring of a carbonated drink over the works.

Liquefied Natural Gas (LNG)

By the mid-1980s upwards of 15 percent of the U.S. gas supply will be provided in the form of liquefied natural gas. Most of the gas will come from Algeria via large tankers to east coast transshipment points. The gas is frozen down to −260° F. in Algeria, shipped, and turned back into gas in the United States.

The gas is highly volatile in its frozen state. No conclusive studies demonstrating safety have ever been carried out. In early studies the Bureau of Mines concluded LNG will explode on contact with water. Thus, a gash in a tanker could set off a large explosion. Another test suggests that gas, escaping from a damaged ship, would float on the wind in an invisible cloud, to be ignited by a cigarette or other spark, setting off a firestorm. Such a gas cloud, flowing from an injured LNG tanker in New York harbor, would float in the west wind over the tip of the city. On ignition it would turn the lower end of Manhattan into a firestorm. Incredulity at such possible damage can be dissipated by studying the LNG disaster that took place in Cleveland in 1944, when a tank of liquid gas exploded. The escaping liquid gas turned the sewers into rivers of flame, which constantly exploded with widescale destruction of property and loss of life (128 casualties).

Scenario No. 5.
Terrorists fire a projectile at an LNG tanker as it proceeds through a populous port. The ship would explode or let off an inflammable gas cloud over population centers nearby. While the Coast Guard provides protection for LNG tankers, it would be impossible to stop an attack of this kind.

Scenario No. 6.
A group of terrorists approach, board, and take command of an LNG tanker, threatening to blow it up in the port of a city such as New York, Boston, Philadelphia, Los Angeles, unless certain demands are met.

Assuming the take-over was close to shore, there is no military means of recovery which would not gravely imperil many hundreds of lives and extensive property. It should be pointed out that since there are no evacuation plans for any city in the United States, it would be impossible to secure the inhabitants in the event of such a threat.

If the terrorists were foolish enough to commandeer an LNG tanker at sea, the tanker could be blown up by plane or submarine. Although the crew would, of course, be lost along with the terrorists, it is of interest to note that most of the LNG tankers are foreign flag vessels, manned by crews of other nations. DOD and State Department should comment on reaction by other nations to military attack.

Smoke

Nuclear Facilities
   The vulnerability of nuclear power plants,
both civil and military, has been examined in a
separate Task Force memorandum. Plutonium
shipments were also examined in this memorandum. It is sufficient here to underline the vulnerability of these plants to groups of determined saboteurs, as demonstrated on a number of
occasions in recent years. Blackhat military
teams have found no difficulty in penetrating
such plants in the course of exercises.
   In terms of their publicity value, nuclear
power plants have always been deemed likely
targets for terrorist assault—even though the
Task Force considers pipeline vulnerability
far graver in implications for security. It
goes without saying that under certain conditions the sabotage of a nuclear plant could result in a major catastrophe. In view of the ongoing clamor and demonstrations over nuclear
power, security measures have already been reviewed and should continue to be so on an ongoing
basis.

Water
   This most basic of energy support systems, essential to life, has grave security implications. The northwestern states are dependent
on electricity created by hydro-power. Coal
mining production on the eastern slopes of the
Rockies also necessitates a steady supply of
water. Water is used in processing coal and also
in the manufacture of synthetic gas. Numerous
synthetic gas plants are either planned or
under construction. Dam vulnerability and se-

curity is under review, as are the possibili-
ties of weather modification (cloud seeding,
etc.) by terrorist groups. Introduction of
toxic substances into urban supply systems is
also under review.

Conclusion
  Energy supply systems on the east coast of the
continental United States, from Washington
through Boston, are vulnerable at almost any
point, to the most amateurish attack. An attack
on the natural gas or LNG supplies to southern
California would also be well within the compe-
tence of any determined group. Oil distribu-
tion in the South is similarly vulnerable.

  Recommendations
* Electricity. An Executive Order requiring
all public and private producing and transmission companies and organizations operating in
interstate commerce to interlink their facilities in a national grid.
* Natural gas. All natural gas pipelines operating in interstate commerce should be re-
quired to interlink with each other in a national grid.
* LNG. It is probably impossible to demonstrate
adequate safety procedures for liquefied natural gas shipments. In the meantime, LNG tankers
should be provided with military escorts while
within U.S. territorial waters.

  General
  It is clear from the foregoing survey that despite procedures recommended above, the United

States government cannot secure the nation
against fuel vulnerability. Though increased
alertness in guarding energy systems must be
implemented, it is clear that the most effective security will be preemptive: a stepped-up
program of intelligence and surveillance of
all potential saboteur and terrorist groups; a
computer bank of all such individuals and
groups; ongoing penetration of their organizations and advance intelligence on their intentions.

A Missed Opportunity

James Schlesinger's special inter-agency meeting to counter nuclear sabotage and contemplate bailout plans for the nuclear industry began somewhat late. Proceedings were delayed by the untimely end of A. Smedley.

At 8 A.M. that morning A. Smedley had been crouching for 45 minutes waiting for his chance and now he saw it coming. Ten flights below, at ground level, the old white Pontiac convertible carrying the Secretary of Energy slid next to the curb and Schlesinger emerged. Smedley tensed, gauged time and distance in a series of rapid mental equations. Two more feet would do it. Schlesinger moved forward.

The time was now. Smedley rose up on the sill of his

Smoke

office window and with one last wild cry launched himself down toward the Secretary.

But Smedley had misjudged the progress of the Secretary, an ardent birdwatcher and, indeed, listener to recordings of birdsong. A small thrush was hopping along the sidewalk and the Secretary paused to observe it. There was a whooshing noise and Smedley struck the pavement with an unpleasant thwonk two feet from the well-shined shoes of his chief.

There was confusion. There were ambulances. There were policemen, agents, doctors, crowds. There were questions. Why had A. Smedley, a 56-year-old career bureaucrat in charge of alternative energy programs under the Assistant Secretary of Energy for the Environment in the DOE, done such a thing?

The note discovered on Smedley's desk was confusing. Wild abuse for the Secretary alternated with expressions of guilt for what Smedley referred to as my "unconscionable acts." Scribbled at the bottom was Smedley's last recorded intention: to "take the Secretary with me."

Only months later did a team from the FBI and the General Accounting Office tentatively establish the truth.

In his capacity as overseer of alternative energy programs Smedley had been known as a keen bureaucratic infighter. He was single and serious. The research contracts he had commissioned produced some of the best work flowing into the Department from outside contractors. Among them, a masterly report showed how the human waste produced in the greater New York area could be recycled to complement usage of natural gas. Another report outlined proposals to create gas from the coalfields in Appalachia, thereby improving on the poverty of the region. A third suggested novel designs for stoves, improving their heating capacity.

Most intriguing of all Smedley's contract work was that to do with research programs in the field of agricultural uses of solar energy. Smedley had let several contracts to a certain Jerome Davis, based in Fresno, California, to study solar energy in drying crops, and to help the habitation of animals. This Davis was noted in the contract literature as a small business farmer with a fine array of academic degrees. His address was a post office box in Fresno, and his output and the contracts had been most impressive, widely cited in the field.

Investigators proceeding to Fresno found the post office box much in arrears on rent. Asking for receipts of previous payments, field agents of the FBI found they had been paid in cash and signed by A. Smedley.

Further investigation of Smedley's travel records established that Smedley, on assignments from the DOE to investigate contract work, had often passed through Fresno and that these trips had coincided with payments made for the post office box. The clerk remembered a man, adorned with dark glasses and wrapped in a scarf on the warmest days.

Checks from the government to Jerome Davis for his contract work had been made out, so the GAO discovered, to Alternative Neo-Energy Systems. The sole officer of Alternative Neo-Energy Systems turned out to be A. Smedley. In the previous three years Alternative Neo-Energy Systems had taken in $2.5 million for contract work with the Department of Energy.

There remained, in this mundane story of Washington life, the puzzle of the high quality of Smedley's work for Smedley. Investigators reviewing the research papers found nothing to question beyond some peculiar side references. One such paper noted a research trip to London involving a two-week voyage by ocean liner. Another had mysterious mentions of a Packard car that had existed 50 years before. Further detective work through the computer bank in the Library of Congress produced the discovery that the work put out by Alternative Energy Systems was in fact that of W.E. Davis, a noted authority on uses of energy who had flourished in the 1920s.

What had Smedley done with the $2.5 million? Further patient work established that Smedley had made out large checks on the Alternative Neo-Energy Systems account to himself, in cash. There the trail seemingly ended, until the post office clerk in Fresno remembered that the man in the dark glasses and scarf had been in the habit of taking out postal orders in $1000 denominations.

In a final report, not communicated to the public, the FBI agent in charge of the case concluded that it was "almost certain" that Smedley had been one of the major anonymous financiers of the anti-nuclear movement for the previous four years.

Smedley's posthumous exposure lay in the future. His intended victim, who had become habituated to threats

A *Missed Opportunity*

on his life in the days when he was purging the CIA for President Nixon, settled comfortably at his desk and pondered the busy day ahead. In profile he seemed like a statue as he gazed imperiously across the realms of his new empire. Only the glowing ember in his trusty briar pipe indicated that behind the impassive facade lay a mind ever pondering the problems of visiting destruction on the United States. The recorded notes of the greater crested grebe flowed melodiously from the tape recorder in the corner of his office. He felt at peace.

Nostalgically he looked at the photographs on his office wall. Mementoes of a glorious career. There was the billowing cloud of dust from the underground nuclear test explosion on Amchitka. Schlesinger stirred excitedly. What glory days those had been at the old AEC! There had been his commitment to the test, the anguished howls of the native population in the Aleutians, his final suggestion to his wife and children to live on Amchitka for the duration of the test. Then the explosion, inaugurating 500,000 years of radiation poisoning of the entire region.

Schlesinger's eyes floated to another portrait: President Nixon swearing him in as head of the CIA. Next to this, another of him standing on an aircraft carrier as Secretary of Defense. Those had been the days; when he and old Rand cronies—more carefree in those happy times—had planned preemptive strikes against the Soviet Union over Sunday brunch. The family had loved those informal war games, shuffling napkin rings, knives, forks, and even plates back and forth across the

table, miming the intoxicating parry and thrust of nuclear combat. There had been those thrilling hours at
the end of Watergate when, with the President beaten
and alone, he had taken over total command of all U.S.
forces. A chance missed, to be sure. It had taken the
combined efforts of the Joint Chiefs, Henry Kissinger,
and Vice-President Ford to deflect him from the
longed-for counterforce strike.

With a start Schlesinger became aware that the
buzzer on his desk had been sounding for some time.

"Yes?"

"The Vice-President, Sir."

With an indulgent smile Schlesinger picked up the
phone.

"Morning, Mr. Vice-President, what can I do for
you?"

Mondale's voice came through, rising to its habitual
plaintive whine.

He had not been informed of the inter-agency Nuke-
Sab meeting. He would like to come to this meeting. It
was his right to come to this meeting. When was the
meeting?

Schlesinger switched the phone to the conference
mode and leaned back in his chair, puffing contentedly
on his pipe. On and on Mondale rambled, as Schlesinger slowly raised the taped birdsong in answer.

"What is our attitude to solar investment tax credit
funding?"

"Tweet, tweet," went the crested warbler.

Mondale sounded uncertain. "Mr. Secretary, is this
line secure? I seem to be hearing bird song."

A Missed Opportunity

Schlesinger lowered the tape and barked into the phone, "Fritz, you are more than welcome to come to all our meetings, and, of course, we will inform you when they occur. My assistant told me that this morning you would be addressing the Denver Chamber of Commerce in Colorado on the matter of the unfortunate dam disaster, not to mention the President's renewed commitment to clear cutting of timber in the west. I assume you are in Denver?"

"As a matter of fact, Mr. Secretary, Air Force One has had some problems in landing, due to the unforeseen presence of demonstrators on the runway. We are presently in a holding pattern over Portland, Oregon. However, this does not alter the fact that it is my right to attend all Nuke-Sab meetings."

"Of course it doesn't, Fritz," Schlesinger said soothingly. "Would you wish us to hold off for 30 minutes or so, in case you wish to attempt a speedy return."

"That will not be necessary."

Carrot and Stick

As Schlesinger laid down the phone his secretary ush-
ered in the members of the inter-agency task force.
There were faces and briefcases from the FBI, the State
Department, the Department of Energy itself, the Pentagon. Puffing behind the rest came a raffish figure in
sneakers, tennis shorts, and sweat-stained T-shirt: Ham
Jordan from the White House.

"Our brief from the President," Schlesinger said
briskly, "was straightforward. The overall threat of the
anti-nuclear movement to our energy plans must be
tempered by the political climate prevailing this year.
Let me put it to you straightforwardly. We want to
crush this movement, but if possible we should do so by
working against it from within. By seduction rather

than ah . . . brutal conquest."

"If I might say so, Sir," the FBI assistant director said modestly, "we have placed all the major figures in the anti-nuclear groups under tight surveillance. Since, in the view of the President's counsel and the Attorney General, these leaders are directly in touch with foreign elements who may wish to prejudice our national security, this surveillance has been established without the need for warrants."

"Excellent."

"As a result I can assure you that it is impossible for these leaders to lay plans without us becoming expeditiously advised of their intentions. We also have a computer interface with the utilities industry and are exchanging information with their security consultants on a regular basis."

"Splendid."

"In view of the Supreme Court's reinterpretation of the Fourth Amendment in 1978 we have outstanding warrants in the event of the need for sudden entry into any of the premises of these extremists."

"Excellent." Schlesinger turned to his own aide in charge of regulatory enforcement.

"General, how are we doing on the political front?"

"Well, Sir, as you know we now have a 3-2 majority on the Nuclear Regulatory Commission. So there's now no problem in getting further plants licensed."

"But," Jordan chimed in, "what happens if your swing vote doesn't hold?"

"In that case," said the aide, brandishing a thick report, "we have an advisory opinion from the President's counsel and the Attorney General that places the propagation of nuclear power within the President's personal control, under the terms of the Emergency Preparedness Act. Legally, he can simply order them to be built."

"Come, come," said Schlesinger. "These are just technicalities, mere maneuvers. What about political relations with the protesters?"

The late A. Smedley's assistant, now handling alternative energy programs, broke in.

"Well, Sir, I'm pleased to announce that your department has recently let two million-dollar contracts for small solar R&D to two protest groups. And with the generous cooperation of the CIA we have persuaded the Saudi Arabian government to commit $25 million for the purpose of introducing solar technology to the underdeveloped portions of the world."

"Yes, yes," said Schlesinger impatiently. "Your point?"

"The CIA suggested, and the Saudis readily agreed, to employ 150 of the leading U.S. environmentalists and anti-nuclear spokesmen as paid consultants and they are now on their way to Riyadh, on the first of a series of monthly visits."

Schlesinger wagged his pipe in casual acknowledgment of the ploy.

"What other actions is the administration taking in this election year to demonstrate its commitment to what our President has called the only truly moral form of energy—the Sun?"

A quiet man wearing thick bifocals piped up from the

Smoke

foot of the table. Schlesinger glanced at the memo in front of him. Clarence Todd: inter-agency co-ordinator of U.S. foreign aid initiatives in the provision of cheap alternative energy to the underdeveloped world.

Todd rummaged in his briefcase and then came up with a poster. He unfurled it proudly. It showed a black man holding up his manacled hands toward a large orange blob in the top right-hand corner of the picture. Beneath it were the words, *Let the Sun Shine In.*

"As you know," Todd explained, "the President feels that his human rights initiatives have been—aside from the intervention of the Rangers in South Yemen last year—one of the more popular strategies of his administration and have won him the respect of peoples round the world.

"It has been our concern to see if the human rights campaign can be linked with the energy strategies of the administration. As you are all aware, the sterility and premature deaths of certain South Pacific islanders as well as Eskimos following our resumption of atmospheric testing have resulted in most unfortunate publicity. In an effort to counter this we have acted on a suggestion of Sam Brown, overall director of the Peace Corps.

"Mr. Brown has advised that the U.S. government should place maximum pressure—along with US AID funding—on certain third world leaders to install solar manufacturing plants in their major correctional facilities, for the prisoners to assemble. I am advised by experts, notably Mr. Gar Alperovitz of the National

Center for Economic Alternatives, that solar power will be a decisive way of guiding some of our less democratic allies toward modernity."

"How," gruffly barked Admiral Grainger, liaison from the Pentagon.

"You see, Sir, solar energy has to be adopted on a geographic basis and is not amenable to economies of scale. Thus, if the countries were to be compelled into decentralized solar-based energy production the centralization which leads to a totalitarian state would be averted in favor of democratic localization."

There was a snort from Grainger and a snapping sound from the head of the conference table as Schlesinger's pipestem broke in his clenched hand. Blindly he reached for the bird song knob and the meeting was engulfed in twittering as he fought to regain his composure. Finally he lowered the volume and spoke again.

"That is the most unutterable rubbish I have ever heard."

Schlesinger watched Todd sadly wrap up his poster and then continued.

"Let me try to clarify matters. For the duration of this year we have to bribe the anti-nuclear movement with compromise, money, and, if necessary, jobs in the administration. Simultaneously we must press forward with plans to crush them by every means permissible within the law as interpreted by the President's chief counsel and the Attorney General."

Schlesinger strolled to the window and watched the remains of A. Smedley being scraped off the sidewalk.

The men filed out, except for Jordan, who sauntered over to him and began to confer with the Secretary and the CIA man in a low murmur. Todd, scurrying out with his disgraced poster, thought he heard the CIA man mutter the single word "zirconium."

Campaign Announcements

The zirconium scandal lay in the dim future. Let us leave it now, burgeoning in the bosoms of the CIA and certain Saudi and Georgian businessmen and turn to the hustle and bustle of spring-time politics in an election year.

By the spring of 1980 advertisements by major corporations had become the preferred means of communicating serious politics to the citizenry. Supreme Court decisions in the previous year had severely curtailed the ability of newspapers to report on events, holding that discussion of political intention and ascription of political motive constituted unwarranted breaches of personal privacy, protected under the Fourth Amendment. However, the Court had recog-

Smoke

nized the First Amendment right of corporations to communicate their views on matters of general and self-interest, and to take tax credits for such communications accordingly.

Thus it was that on May 4, 1980, the following announcement appeared in major newspapers across the country and—read by distinguished actors—on network television and radio.

Politics and the Rational Mind
THE ENEMY WITHIN

Let's face it. Our leaders have let us down. America is a great country and we've been the first to proclaim it. But sometimes, frankly, we feel all alone. Why?

For the last four years we in the business community have tried to make some honest suggestions about what is wrong with this country. We've told you how the government throttles productivity, how it destroys initiative. And we've argued that the overzealous regulators in Washington are making our problems harder to solve.

Excuse our bluntness. President Carter did his best. He introduced in Congress an energy plan which had some good points, and he showed us he was a statesman in freeing gas prices, but we are no nearer Energy Independence than we were four years ago.

Now a word about the nay-sayers. The governor of California would have us believe that solar energy can replace oil, natural gas, coal, and nuclear power. It's a beautiful idea, but take our word for it; it won't work. Ralph Nader (who elected him any-

Campaign Announcements

way?) and his eco-lytes squawk about the evils of "Big Business" and the "Special Interests."

Well, we think he must be talking about us. Yes, we have a special interest. That special interest is YOU, the consumers and producers of America. And we think the nay-sayers are trying to lead you astray. If it were not for Big Business there wouldn't be any natural gas to light your stoves, any oil to run your car, any electricity to heat and light your homes.

Pardon our impertinence, but we think we have every right to tell you the programs and people we think are good for this country in this election year. Like you, we want to hear what the candidates have to say. We haven't made up our minds yet. But we think you should know about an Enemy Within. You'll be hearing from this enemy in the months ahead.

This Enemy Within wears many disguises. He comes in the blue jeans of an anti-nuclear demonstrator. He is sometimes the so-called "whistleblower" in government. He is sometimes the so-called "reformer" in local politics. He is for "good government." He is a professor, a high school teacher, a labor organizer.

Listen to what he says. He is for more regulation. He wants big government to tell YOU what to do. He wants to control YOUR lives.

Most dangerously he is rallying citizens like you against Energy Independence by opposing nuclear power. And he is helping the Enemy Without by calling for nuclear disarmament. Now, we happen to know something about nuclear power. It's part of our business. We think nuclear power is a good thing. And we want you to know that we are going to

· 5 5 ·

fight back against the Enemy Within. We want you to join us in this fight.

VOTE FOR NUCLEAR POWER. Make sure your candidates, whoever they may be, support a rational energy program for the United States.

Join us in finding and fighting the Enemy Within. Share with us your information. For details of what nuclear power can mean for you and your families, and for advice, call this toll-free number: 800–555–8080.

The Conscience of the Rich

In the first weekend of June both Jack and Julie flew to California for a summit meeting between leaders of the anti-nuclear movement and their main financial backers.

Little known to the general public, but all-important to many radical causes was the association of young heirs to some of America's largest fortunes, jocularly referred to as URF or Union of Rich Folk. URF had first come together in the tempest of the Vietnam war, prompted and pushed forward by the 21-year-old heiress to the Piano Trust, Regina Harbury. Since then, meeting in deepest secrecy in different parts of the country, URF had helped to finance major programs for social change, from time to time recruiting fresh assets in the shape of new millionaire members.

It was URF which had seeded radical feminism, sponsored legalization of marijuana, campaigned for solar energy, initiated the Program for Honesty in the Defense Budget, and lobbied in boardrooms for divestiture of U.S. corporate asets in South Africa. But most important, since 1972 URF members had poured millions of dollars into the attack on nuclear energy.

To the casual investigator these millions would seem to have come from separate liberal foundations, all obeying the laws of the land and pursuing their independent paths of good work. Not so. The decision of what was to be spent where was made by the URF group, gathering twice yearly in their secret conclaves and then handing edicts for disbursement to the foundation directors.

Jack and Julie, a little spacey from a quaalude-sodden flight across the continent, emerged blinking into the dry heat of the Central Valley. As they stood outside the terminal a girl with long blonde hair stuck her head out a blue van and motioned for them to get in. After a half hour's ride through the flat farm land around Sacramento they entered a forest of almond trees and then emerged into a clearing, in the middle of which was situated a spacious ranch.

The ranch complex, belonging to a Silver Trust heir, was, they soon learned, totally self-sufficient, replete with fishponds, recycled sewage systems, solar collectors, and, of course, the clivus mulchum toilets on whose behalf Abby Rockefeller had expended so much money and effort. There was nothing spartan about the ranch. Whirlpool baths, solar-heated swimming pools vied for the eye with extensive tennis courts, umbrageous jogging paths, and a succulent acre of French bio-dynamic garden. The dirt looked good enough to eat. Paraquat-free marijuana flourished in the back forty, horses neighed in the paddock, and kine lowed in the milking shed. Hens crouched over vast organic eggs.

Here were gathered the progeny of names famous in American industrial history, children—many of them approaching middle age—who had for so many years worked together in the cause of social justice.

At one end of the ranch complex, the URF complement now gathered to discuss their strategy, meeting behind closed doors, protected by a trim female Zen guide. Elsewhere the activists who had been called to California from all around the country chatted idly about tactics and strategies.

Within the closed room, John Challis, heir to the Bauxite Trust, reported on his recent meeting with Dick Brownlees, a young prominent member of Carter's staff and himself a descendant of the Banana Family, at the Top of the World restaurant in New York. Challis, who passed his time as a small business consultant, often devoting his energies to educating public interest groups in the theories of Adam Smith, had not seen Brownlees since their days together at prep school. So he was somewhat surprised at the sudden call and request for a meeting.

At the Top of the World, Brownlees, munching quails' eggs, had made it clear that the White House and Carter himself were anxious to convey to the conferees in California that the government was serious in its support of solar energy and would work seriously with them toward implementing a meaningful solar program. Challis was shocked that Brownlees knew of the URF meeting, but he said nothing. Challis had indicated, speaking in a rather abstract manner, that there was little enthusiasm among the environmental community for dealing with the President.

A murmur of agreement ran around the room as Challis said these words.

"I told him that speaking frankly we thought, that is the environmental community thought, Schlesinger was a double crosser and could not be trusted."

"So what did he say to that?"

"Brownlees insisted the President was serious. He grew agitated, waved his hands. He said the President wanted a truce, that he would name a new task force."

"Sure, we've heard that before. There was a task force in '76, one in '78, and now another?"

"Wait a moment," Challis continued, "Brownlees claimed he was there to cut a deal. They would name a task force and use that as the means to support solar energy. For our part, we would agree to stop funding new arenas of nuclear protest."

"New arenas," piped up a young woman in the rear. "What's that mean?"

Challis waited a moment for silence to be restored. "He gave me to understand that we're to stop financing direct action. Brownlees said Carter knew, they all knew, that nuclear power was doomed because of the

economics. Lovins was right on that score. But there
were outstanding commitments. He would not go into
these commitments, but asked me to understand that
they do exist."

Once again the room fell silent.

"Let's get this clear. They're suggesting that we hold
off funding new attacks? They're suggesting that we not
support groups dedicated to civil disobedience. No
more money to the Quakers or groups associated with
them?"

"Exactly," Challis paused to take a handful of nuts.
"That's what Brownlees said. What worries Carter most
is massive direct action. Threats of violence."

"What do we get out of this?" came a cynical shout
from the back of the room.

Challis cleared his throat. "Let's be rational. This is
our moment of maximum purchase on the system.
Right? I had the impression that Carter, that his people,
really are serious about solar power. Brownlees as good
as told me Schlesinger's days are numbered.

"And that once they get past this problem of former
commitments to the nuclear industry, then support for
solar will be an administration priority."

"I find this hard to believe," said Janice of the Cookie
Trust. "Anyway who are we to make policy for all these
people? Why shouldn't they have a chance to say for
themselves what they want to do? After all we do call
it a movement."

"And it is a movement," piped up the heir to the
Mailhouse Fortune.

"Let's be sensible about this," said a Railroad bar-

Smoke

onet. "There is a sense in which we are elitist. And we decided that because we by accident of birth had some extra resources, we would use them in a good way. I'm all for it—but we might as well recognize ourselves for what we are. The alternative would be to give all our money to the government. And I'm not going to do that." He paused, taking a nourishing drink of carrot juice. "If we pull back from supporting direct action at Indian Point and other sites over the next few months, and really get a commitment for solar, then it's worth the trouble. And let's be serious about this. We have to make the decision—not the groups we finance. We have the money and the power and that's why the President is talking to us, not them."

"You really turn me off," said a lissome representative of the Newspaper Trust. "I think what you say is wretched." And with that she rushed from the room sobbing.

"She's right, she's right," cried Bert Barnschild of the Carpet Monopoly. "These are real people we're talking about. Do we believe in meaningful social change or don't we?"

Up spoke Rollo Lamston, heir to the Soybean Fortune. "I agree with Cindy. We don't have a right to dictate the movement's attitude. But I do see a point in these conversations with the White House. The President can't talk to everyone. There are real politics involved in this. And let me put another thought in your heads. If we cooperate with the White House venture —or even look as though we are—it will put more pressure on Jerry Brown to move a little faster here in

·62·

The Conscience of the Rich

California. So it's a two-edged sword."

A murmur of approval ran around the group, as chopsticks dipped energetically into bowls of soggy brown rice.

"What will I tell my lover?" asked Darlene Laffor of the Diamond Family. "Ron's just a construction worker. He hates nuclear power because he thinks it bad for people. He wants to take part in direct action. He's even talked to me about taking over a plant. Are you asking me to manipulate him?"

Rollo edged over and put his arm comfortingly around Darlene's shoulders.

"You're not manipulating Ron. We're not asking you to do that. And I know you wouldn't ask me to manipulate Alice. But remember, you have a commitment to us just as much as you do to him. And we have a commitment to one another. There is power in numbers and we have to remember that."

Amid tears and hugs, unity was finally reestablished. Exhausted from the prolonged debate the heirs and heiresses took a break.

Pastoral Symphony

Darlene wandered out to the mulching shed. Rollo was waiting for her as she knew he would be.

Together they eyed the great mounds of steaming compost.

"You've come too early," said Rollo, letting his hand rest lightly upon her shoulder. "You should see our melons. You must come back later for the harvest."

It was hot in the mulching shed, as the rich, heavy, always exhilarating odor of cow dung warmed their nostrils.

There was a lowing noise from further up the shed. "That's Betsy," said Rollo in an affectionate tone. Hip brushing hip, they wandered up the shed. Darlene barely heard Rollo's learned discourse about organic milk. Her head was spinning from the effects and excitements of the long day's discussion.

"Rollo," she said softly.

"What?"

She looked at him with an air of direct invitation. Rollo, flushing slightly, reached down past the furry thighs and grasped the cow's udder with a practiced hand.

"You see," said Rollo, grasping Betsy's long, rubbery teat. "You learn by experience. Do you want to try?"

Darlene leaned forward over Rollo's shoulder and grasped another udder.

"Now watch what I do."

A rippling motion went through his wrist and knuckles and a jet of warm milk splashed on Darlene's bare feet. Darlene jerked at her udder. Nothing happened. Squirt after squirt came from the udder Rollo was now manipulating with increasing zeal.

Darlene yanked and pulled, but the udder still remained limp and dry. Seconds turned into minutes. Sweat streamed into her eyes. The heat and scents weighed on her brain, ate at her senses as she felt Rollo laboring beside her. It seemed to Darlene that she was climbing a high mountain. The more she climbed, the further the peak. Yes, then in an instant, yes, now, maybe the quickening. Here, now, yes, yes, she is, yes. A thin trickle, a thicker stream, then the steady sluicing of milk from her udder. Like the music of the spheres, twin streams chimed against the pail's side.

Pastoral Symphony

Julie and Jack had enjoyed their afternoon in the sun, renewing old acquaintanceships and forging new ones. Julie passed around copies of the now widely circulated FBI memorandum on fuel supply interdiction and squeals of delight arose as they pondered which parts of the United States could be paralyzed first. All agreed it was a tie between New York and Los Angeles.

Challis emerged from the ranch house and stood uneasily at the edge of the pool. Silence slowly fell.

At first he had some difficulty in explaining the attitude of the URF executive to direct action and began to stutter under a volley of indignant abuse and accusations of sell-out.

Then the spirit which had make the Bauxite Trust what it was entered his sinews and stiffened his resolve.

"I don't think you're quite hearing me. I know you are independent people, and we wouldn't have you otherwise. Let's just say we agree to disagree, at least for the time being. We in URF feel very strongly about violence and to be honest with you, we feel very strongly about our country. We feel we have to give the President a chance. Our commitment to all the programs we have so far been funding remains as strong as it ever was."

Challis paused. "But we will not be financing any direct action the rest of this year."

Teresa O'Rourke, leader of the Seattle Direct Action Committee, cut across the mounting clamor.

"I might as well say what I've thought all along. You

guys are for shit. You always have been, and you always will be."

Challis remained calm. "Thank you for sharing your anger with me, Teresa. We respect you and we love you."

The activists were settling down for a lengthy argument when a small bus, driven by the Zen guide, suddenly appeared from behind the mulching shed and stopped in front of the ranch house.

"Well," said Challis, "I guess you folks better be getting along. Thanks for coming." Bauxite turned and rejoined other fortunate Minerals and Industrial Products within. In sullen, disappointed silence the activists clambered aboard the bus.

On the way back to Sacramento indignation gave way to determined scheming. Plans for direct action would be stepped up. A coordinating committee to plan action for the Democratic Convention in Seattle was formed. Teresa was placed in charge.

The bus fairly shook with passion and plans as it proceeded back toward the airport outside Sacramento. To the south, in Los Angeles, similar hopes and dreams boiled up in the brain of a young politician laying his own plans for the Convention.

Jerry Brown, asleep in his modest apartment, was having the dream, which on so many nights and days had turned into a nightmare.

Jerry Brown's Nightmare

Yes, in the summer of 1980 Jerry Brown slept, and as he slept he dreamed and lo! in his dream he saw a gaily painted bus, wending its way around Dupont Circle in Washington, D.C., closely followed by the black limousines and station wagons of the Secret Service. Snow softly drifted down in the raw Christmas morning. The man slouched in the back paid little attention to the waves of the passersby. Ever since the austere Zen ceremony of his inauguration, President Jerry Brown had made just such a commuting journey twice a day from his simple basement flat in Mount Pleasant.

His face momentarily tightened as the bus passed one of his most noted initiatives, the Pillory for Idle Bureaucrats in Lafayette Square. There they stood, shivering

Smoke

in the chill breeze: six civil servants accused by anonymous complaint of slack performance and condemned
to a week in the stocks.

As President Brown strode through the corridors of
the White House, his restless mind probed the problems ahead and the crises that confronted his young
administration. They would be waiting for him in the
Cabinet room, and the President sighed at the thought
of the long hours of deliberation that lay ahead.

He hesitated, then entered crisply and took his seat
at the center of the long table, glancing at the worried
faces of his closest advisers. He motioned to Scoop Jackson, Secretary of Defense, for an update on the revolt.

"We've got problems, Jerry," Jackson said. "It looks
like a full-scale revolt. The whole of the Midwest is on
strike and it's spreading down to the Southern Rim.
Auto mechanics, public workers, shopkeepers, even
journalists. It's really an uprising by small business. And
there's worse. Army and National Guard units have
refused to move. This morning I ordered the arrest of
army commanders in both the South and the Middle
West. Since then we've lost contact."

Brown nodded tautly, then turned to his Attorney
General, Mitchell Rogovin.

"Mitch?"

"The paramilitary units are intact, but frankly we're
not sure how reliable they are."

A monkish figure at the foot of the table broke in.
"Too much outwardness, Jerry. Keep it flowing." It was
Swami Shearer, head of the Zen Awareness Project and

the President's closest and most respected spiritual adviser.

"I am that which is both inward and outward," the President answered softly. A worried murmur swelled up in the room and Brown signalled sharply for silence. But his impetuous Secretary for Transport, Tom Hayden, would not be stilled.

"Jerry, what are we going to do?"

"What we have always done. Have no plan. See what happens. Adapt to circumstances."

"But, Mr. President," burst in Secretary of Labor Jesse Jackson. "The country's breaking apart."

"Maybe that's a good thing. Maybe it isn't," muttered the President petulantly as he rose and stood gazing out of the window, brooding on the recent past. It had all seemed to be going so well. The successful crusade against the Carter administration; the hundred days of Austerity; welfare programs cancelled; space colonies launched; decisive suppression of food riots in the Northeast; a tussle with the last remnants of American heavy industry as it switched headquarters to the Caribbean, joining the banks and insurance companies already based there. Why the revolt? There was work for all, all who deserved it and all willing to accept the Brown Maximum Wage Plan—$1 an hour.

He turned back and surveyed the table. One chair was empty. That of Felix Rohatyn, Secretary of the Treasury and Brown's roving troubleshooter. Late the previous evening Rohatyn had appeared at the door of the President's apartment, interrupting his meditation.

Rohatyn had brusquely outlined for him the seriousness of the situation but informed him that he had a rescue plan in mind. All he needed was 24 hours.

The time was almost up.

Three thousand miles away Rohatyn was walking barefoot through the Pacific surf. It was barely dawn. At his side strode a familiar figure.

"Mr. Rohatyn, I swore I would never return."

"You have to," riposted Rohatyn. "The country needs you. You need only go to Los Angeles. There the train is ready. Crowds are already being assembled across the country. Millions upon millions of people await your passage. Never in history has there been a time like this. Only you can save the country."

Still the old man hesitated, as he had always done before a big decision, retreating into himself as he pondered the options.

Back in Washington, Secretary of State Richard Holbrooke tensely awaited the phone call. Late in the afternoon it came.

"Felix?"

"He'll do it."

Quickly Holbrooke put down the phone. A minute later he was talking to Mary McGrory, the President's press secretary, arranging for the great news to be leaked to *The Washington Post*—the only newspaper, despite the nationwide industrial unrest, that was still being published by a workforce battered into submission by draconian management.

The rest was history. The great comeback train wending its way across the country. Brown's famous response, when Rohatyn finally broke the news to him late that Christmas evening. "Truth has two sides." And of course, the climactic moment of return at Union Station.

They had all been there, some of them weeping openly. Old Arthur Burns fondly clasping the hand of his former master. Ehrlichman and Haldeman, beaming in welcome and forgiveness. Erect James Schlesinger. Portly Pat Moynihan. Eager Joe Kraft. And, crying softly to himself at the back of the mighty throng, John Mitchell. Only Henry Kissinger was missing, torn apart some months before by angry Japanese students at Narita airport as he had attempted mediation.

In the glare of the television lights the old man slowly raised his arms in a familiar gesture, and, just before Jerry awoke, it seemed that Nixon's nose was getting longer and longer and longer as it reached out across the land and wrapped itself around his neck.

Town Meeting

President Carter had taken off his jacket and was standing rather shiftily on the gym stage of Allentown Pennsylvania High School. It was his thirty-seventh town meeting of the year. After the Supreme Court decision on privacy and the discontinuation of White House briefings the press had been wary about interrogating the President and the citizens of Allentown were left to their own devices.

They gazed suspiciously at the rubbery features of the Commander in Chief. The questioning was polite but fierce.

"Mr. President," said a formidable-looking lady, "four years ago you promised us that you would end the welfare mess. But there are just as many welfare cheats

Smoke

now as there were then. Why haven't you done anything?"

"I introduced to the Congress the most far-reaching
program in the history of this nation to rid us of welfare
cheats. I believe that white women should be with their
families. We need more children, not less."

The President, scenting some confusion in his audience, paused before continuing. "There are powerful
vested interests in the Congress opposed to my plan.
Certain labor leaders have been working very actively,
some of them under investigation by our Justice Department. I have spoken very frankly to Senator
Kennedy about this obstruction. Like you I am still
waiting for some clear answers."

There was a cry from the back of the hall as a young
woman clutching a young baby sprang up.

"Look at this utility bill," she cried, gesturing at the
piece of paper jammed in the baby's mouth. "$400, and
it's not even winter."

Skin crinkled at the corners of the Commander in
Chief's eyes. Disciplined muscles jerked lips apart and
white teeth briefly gleamed.

"My wife Rosalynn says the same thing to me each
month. With your permission I would like to pass your
bill along to Jim Schlesinger, who runs our nation's energy policy. I'll ask him to aggressively scrutinize your
bill and give you a full explanation."

The President waited while a Secret Service man
hastened to jerk the evidence of extortion from the
youngster's mouth and then raised his hand for extra
emphasis.

Town Meeting

"I have had many such complaints from the American people in the course of this campaign. I want to tell you one thing I have learned as President. There is a second government trying to run this country. It is made up of big shot crooks, fat cats in Wall Street, highly paid doctors, and big time lawyers. I intend to do something about this. We need to restore competition to the market place and make government honest."

Carter stopped. "All this I pledge to you," he said rather mysteriously.

"Meestair Jimmee, Meestair Jimmee," called a short thick-set man in the front row. "I am being called Kemal Yousuff. And I am asking you for my people and maaany meellions also of other peoples, why is it that the United States which these peoples are trusting is not saying No to Israel and its aggression. I am speaking specifically about what Israeli government and gang of robbers are saying to be temporary settlements in southern Turkey. These are what maaany peoples are calling criminal acts and—"

The President cut him short and gazed sternly into the network cameras.

"Our support of the state of Israel is total, absolute, eternal, and without equivocation. I have made this clear on many occasions. I have been assured by our friends in Israel that these settlements are purely for temporary security and that they will accept the substitution of a UN peace-keeping force."

"But Meestair Jimmeee," Yousuff broke in excitedly.

"I think that young man over there has a question," smiled the President, pointing to a high school student.

Smoke

"Mr. President," Jon Dorfman, editor of the Allentown High School paper, said tremulously. "You have been winning in the primaries, but the turnout has been very low. Your support appears to be declining. In view of his own popularity in the polls would you consider substituting Teddy Kennedy for Walter Mondale as your running mate? And if so, do you have reason to believe he would accept?"

"Fritz Mondale is probably the most magnificent vice president in the history of our country. He is my chief of staff and a man with whom I am intimate. I have never attached much importance to polls, any more than Senator Kennedy, one of the most distinguished senators we have today. The Senator has often assured me that in view of personal family problems he wishes to dedicate himself to serving his party, his President, and his nation in the senate. I honor that commitment."

The strategy session later that evening was held in somewhat constricted conditions. Rafshoon had fixed up for the President to stay with a coal miner's family an hour outside Pittsburgh. The presidential helicopter had dropped him down in a field outside Moundsville, West Virginia, where he proceeded by limousine directly to the union hall, where frank exchanges about his invocation of Taft-Hartley in the 1978 coal strike took place. His promise to proceed "expeditiously" on mine safety reform and his moving denunciation of black lung and the big shot coal operators, along with his humorous deprecation of solar energy had won some hearts and minds. As he clamped on his miner's hat he was satisfied to hear a moderately robust ovation.

Later that night, after his host had departed for the midnight shift and the rest of the family had gone to bed, Carter held a whispered conversation with Pat Caddell in the toolshed, a colloquy interrupted by the occasional scrunch of Secret Service agent Blostak as he patrolled the roof.

They reviewed the day, the President still enthusing on the reception to his populist rampages in the high school and the miners' hall.

"Jimmy," interjected Caddell. "I think we have a serious problem. I've just been speaking to Cambridge Research and although they have not totally tabulated the new survey it's clear enough that your ratings have not improved substantially."

"How about Kennedy? How about the Chappaquiddick factor?"

"Not as potent as we'd hoped. We ran a multiple choice question for younger voters. They were asked whether Chappaquiddick was an island, a woman, a native American or the winner of the Kentucky Derby. 47 percent thought it was the winner of the last Derby. Only 12 percent identified it properly."

"Oh."

"In fact Kennedy's margins have held remarkably stable. And Brown is beginning to show signs of making inroads. He's cutting into your base. And what the poll shows is that people are not convinced by your positions in a few areas: jobs, defense, the Middle East, the environment, inflation, business, labor, agriculture, housing, urban policy, taxation, consumer affairs, veterans, civil service reform, crime, illegal immigration, free trade, and, most of all, energy. They just don't know where you stand."

There was a creak from the roof as Blostak pressed his little recording device against the shingle. Caddell lowered his voice.

"Energy is the big problem. What our polls show is that you are winning neither one of two important constituencies. Particularly after your recent speeches big business feels let down. For example I was talking to one of my clients, the chairman of Westinghouse, the other day. I've been telling them all along that you are committed to a nuclear energy program. Now they're not so sure."

The President stirred petulantly. "Why? Lipshutz saw them just the other day. They surely know the realities of the situation."

Caddell raised a hand. "As regards the other big constituency—the anti-nuclear activists, consumers, Naderites, and so on. This is the nearest we have at the moment in this country to a mass middle class radical movement. I heard yesterday that the White House has been fooling with some deal with the URF, the young rich people. That's crazy. They can't deliver anything. We're going to get their money anyway. Getting them involved in active politics is madness.

"No. The strategy of trying to appeal to all constituencies is simply not going to work this time around. We must have some substance instead of style, Mr. President. We have to realize one thing your friend Ralph Nader has said over and over again: the most effective grass roots political organizations in this country are private corporations. Every time you attack big business, every time you talk about solar energy and make a play for these environmentalists your rating with business goes down. And you have to remember that it is business which organizes labor. It's business that has now organized the blacks. That's what the NAACP experience showed.

"Whatever you may think personally, the nuclear power issue is a symbol for business, for labor, and for the blacks. You don't have to do a great deal to implement nuclear power. But you do have to be decisive in attacking blackmail by radicals, in confronting threats to sabotage energy independence.

"We can turn the situation around. You have got to make people realize that environmentalists are troublemakers. You've got to stop attacking business. Instead you have to support the positive things business has done. Read the Mobil ads. They've got a better sense of what this country is about than anyone else. Each one is an outline for a speech.

"Now, as for action. Stop rewarding these environmentalists with government contracts and grants. Start putting that money into the hands of minorities, blacks, chicanos, women where it will pay off in terms of real votes."

The President had listened alertly, making a few notes on his yellow legal pad. "Pat, can you present this to me in the form of a memorandum, and speak to Ham and Jody and Mr. Kirbo about a new schedule of speeches. Let's talk tomorrow morning.

"I'll start to tilt the other way soon." The President rose. Together they walked out and eyed the half moon.

"You know, Pat," said the President with emotion, "Kennedy has never done one thing to help me. I can stand Brown, though I don't like him. But those Kennedys, they won't even take telephone calls. If there's one thing I'd like to do, it's to screw that sonofabitch."

And Then It Was Dark

It was hot that summer night. The stench from the chemical plants lay heavily on the city of Wilmington. The filthy waters of the Delaware River lay sullen beneath a thick starless sky.

Forty miles to the north, in the electric utility computer complex at Valley Forge five figures in stocking masks with guns in hand barked instructions at terrified computer technicians.

On the outskirts of Wilmington, in the National City Hospital, Nurse Eunice Smathers was administering an enema to Robert Bodkin, handsome patient, stalwart football player. She sensed the unmistakable hum of the hospital's own backup generators coming on line. The lights blinked.

Smoke

At Scrums Gigantic Discount Store, on Route 121, there was a shriek of alarm as the lights went out, cash registers jammed, and exactly 32 percent of the customers began removing goods from the shelves and thrusting them into their pockets.

In the lovely old frame homes along Walnut Street where lived the cream and pride of the Wilmington legal profession air conditioners died, television sets fell silent, darkness came, and families gathered round transistor radios.

It was 9:37 P.M. at State Police headquarters. Commander Ryan was munching a ham and Swiss on a hard roll while he reviewed surveillance reports on his daughter's new boyfriend. The phone rang.

"Commander," a shaken voice said from the other end. "It looks as though we've got a major incident in Wilmington. The lights are out and something funny has happened at PJM headquarters. We're trying to get the Pennsylvania State Police to find out what's happened."

"You're kidding," said Ryan, straining up in his chair to look out the window. Darkness was where Wilmington once glowed. "By God, you're right."

He took another bite on his hard roll. "Hmbbbe mmmhay hmmn?"

"What?"

Ryan swallowed his mouthful. "Where is PJM anyway? What's that got to do with Wilmington?"

"Sir," said a somewhat reproachful voice. "PJM is the control center for all the utilities on the east coast. It's located in Valley Forge."

And Then It Was Dark

Inside the PJM headquarters all was chaos. The night shift technicians had been taken entirely by surprise when the five intruders, dressed in the uniforms of vending machine delivery men, leaped through the door, and slammed it shut behind them.

"This is it," shouted the leader, brandishing a machine pistol. The technicians were quickly trussed and gagged and told to lie face down on the floor. The five went to work with considerable efficiency. It took them just five minutes to isolate the power supply controls for the city of Wilmington. It alone, throughout all the mid-Atlantic states, received their devotion. While four bent over the computer terminals, tapping out the instructions to shut down the electricity to Wilmington, a fifth placed a call to the city's largest all news radio station.

"This is the Nuclear Faction. We are tired of legal mumbo-jumbo. We want nuclear power stopped now. We're shutting down Wilmington, just to show you what can be done. Wilmington today, Philadelphia tomorrow, New York the day after."

Such at least was what the message taken down in shorthand by a flustered receptionist at the radio station and later bannered in the press.

The five left as rapidly as they had arrived. Within half an hour the State Police had freed the technicians. Resetting transmission devices and restoring interconnections to Wilmington took another eleven hours.

The blackout lasted thirteen hours in all. It cost the

city of Wilmington $1.5 million in property damage from looting, lost industrial production, and damage suits.

Three nights later a Cessna 172 swooped down on the desert 200 miles outside the city limits of Los Angeles. Three persons alighted with maps, flashlights, and shovels and looked for markers left the day before.

It took 45 minutes to scrape away the sand and expose the artery of the main natural gas pipeline leading from the Southwest to Los Angeles.

The Cessna had already been in the air again for five minutes when half a dozen rattlesnakes and one prairie dog in the immediate vicinity observed a bright flash. The earth trembled and a sheet of flame shot skyward as natural gas, value $2 per thousand cubic feet, exploded and burned.

A few minutes later subsiding pressure in the pipeline manifested itself in Los Angeles. Oil refineries began to shut down. Stoves and gas-fed air conditioners and refrigerators went out of service. Industries and utilities which had converted to natural gas to reduce air pollution were knocked out of commission.

Within an hour the Los Angeles police were in touch with the FBI, which in turn, following prearranged procedures, had called in the Inter-Agency Task Force on Energy. This top-secret high level group, lodged in the Department of Energy, was in close touch with the CIA, FBI, Nuclear Regulatory Commission, and the Pentagon's Office of Civil Preparedness. Members of the Task Force convened forthwith in their headquarters in Rosslyn, just across the river from Washington and close by the CIA headquarters in Langley.

Soon the task force was scrutinizing maps of the pipeline system. Air traffic controllers in the western states were alerted to be on the lookout for unidentified small aircraft. Satellite reconnaissance of all pipeline systems leading into California was immediately initiated. Specially-trained Rangers attached to the Immigration Service's Border Patrol were parachuted into the sabotage area.

The injured pipe was sealed, and spare sections dropped by helicopter. Gas pipefitters were rushed to the scene. Gas from the northern part of the state was increased in volume and by dawn some industries in the Los Angeles area were beginning to operate on a near to normal basis. Within three days new pipe had been laid and the gas flow was normal.

But there was no trace of the saboteurs.

In his report to Hamilton Jordan, the head of the Task Force, Ambassador Hinckle, after extolling the "swift response" of his own group, made a number of grim points. One, it now seemed clear, in the wake of the PJM and Los Angeles interdictions, that someone had leaked a copy of the Task Force report on fuel supply systems to terrorist groups. Two, that the fuel supply systems in the United States were, as these two incidents had shown, vulnerable to those most primitive forms of assault. Three, that though security measures must now be taken "wherever feasible," especially in large population centers, it was evidently impossible to protect fuel supplies within the continental United States from further assaults.

"To mount tolerable security of fuel supplies," Ambassador Hinckle concluded, "would require an investment as massive as that undertaken during World War II to counteract the German U-boat menace. At that time, it will be recalled, the United States constructed two immense pipelines connecting the oil-producing fields of Texas with the East Coast, thus obviating the necessity of vulnerable intercoastal tanker traffic. It is these very pipes, among others, that are now threatened from within."

Fun and Games at Camp David

Ham and Jody were skeet shooting in Camp David when the Secret Service man told them the President was ready to start the meeting. Settling into the plush chairs they presented a colorful crew: Jimmy in his new flared French jeans, with tennis shirt by Jean of New York; Jody in a St. Laurent après ski; and Ham in Sunny Surplus jeans and Vietnam Vet Shirt. Ham with his usual sartorial wit had retained the World War I gas mask dangling on his khaki belt and Jody wore an Iron Cross and bent hairpins from Punkadelic. Round their necks gleamed spent 30 cal. silver bullets suspended on rusty iron chain. Pat Caddell, ever the jokester, was in the burnoose sent him by a waggish William Safire recalling Caddell's one-time business relationship with Saudi Arabia.

They waited, inhaling occasional pinches of snuff, now fashionable in the White House, and chatting idly about how to cover up the looming zirconium scandal. Powell, with appropriate mimicry, read aloud Hedrick Smith's latest "News Analysis" in *The New York Times.* The President riffled through the minutes of the last Trilateral meeting and nodded appreciatively over David Rockefeller's covering letter.

"These Rockefellers certainly get around," he remarked to no one in particular. "Here's David telling me that he has just had personal conversations with Prime Minister Desai."

"You mean the piss drinker?"

"Yes, Jody, and anyway, David says that Desai says that he wants some more enriched uranium. In fact David says we should get onto it right away. The Indians can't pay for it of course, but David says that his bank will buy it from us at a discount and then he can lease the uranium to Desai. David says this kind of thing is done all the time. I guess he must know. Will you keep an eye on this, Ham?"

"Sure thing, Jimmy." Ham scribbled a note on his yellow scratch pad and stuffed it into his gas mask.

At last they heard the noise they had been waiting for. There was a whirl of helicopter blades, a flurry of Secret Service men, and then an eruption as though a tornado had burst into the room.

"Bert!" the cry went up.

Bert Lance waved in greeting, moving his hand with

some difficulty, since enormous gold rings adorned each finger, weighing them down.

"Gee Bert, you look terrific," said Jimmy in shy greeting, overawed as always by the self-possession and beaming joie de vivre of his old comrade.

"I feel terrific," bellowed Bert. "This is the life. Only yesterday we were tying up a deal in the New Hebrides; Zurich for dinner last night with you know who, and breakfast this morning in Grand Cayman. Just call me Mr. Offshore."

The minutes seemed to fly by as Bert held them rapt with his traveller's tales of bridging loans arduously negotiated, of interim financing brilliantly achieved. In his words breathed the mysteries of the Orient, of Switzerland, and the whole magic world of international finance.

At last, with a sigh of regret, the President remarked that serious matters awaited their attention.

"I wanted to wait till Bert got here, before Pat made his presentation."

"I think it's pretty clear," Caddell began, "that the events in Wilmington and Los Angeles are forcing our hand." He quickly ran through the analysis he had given the President in Moundsville and then added, "Now's the time to move. This nation is being threatened from within. For you to make any kind of play for the environmental vote now will be just like treason."

"I don't know, Pat," said the President unhappily. "I don't want to sound like Nixon after Kent State, and just be upstaged by the Republicans and lose on both ends."

"Oh fuck 'em," Bert burst out. "Screw the bastards to the wall. I always told you, Jimmy. Your friends are and always have been in the business world. Not with these pimply-faced faggot commies and their dike girl friends."

The President winced at Lance's exuberant vocabulary.

"Why Bert, many of them are superb young people, committed to the United States' best interest."

"Bullshit, Jimmy. They will drag you down. Here's what I suggest. Mel Thompson has the right idea. Every time one of those creeps starts demonstrating near a power plant, arrest him and throw him in jail. At the same time arrest the ringleaders, get Griffin to charge them with conspiracy, and just to rub it in, get one of those public interest lawyers down there in the Justice Department to run the case. Have grand jury investigations in every federal courthouse, looking into the possibility of Communist subversion of our fuel supplies and energy program. Shut these bastards up once and for all."

There was a brief silence.

"That sort thing doesn't fly any more," Caddell said sadly. "You can't get away with that." He sighed. "I have to fight this kind of nostalgia every day, when I talk to my clients in industry."

"I think Pat's reasoning is right," Powell opined. "But there's another way of getting to the same objective. Suppose Jimmy takes a low posture on nuclear. When he's asked he'll just continue to say he's got some reservations. But he'll also say we've got to move ahead.

Fun and Games at Camp David

Jimmy's a Democrat so he can say there is a great debate inside the administration about what to do. And that as President he will ultimately make a decision which will be his and his alone, based on all the evidence and that he will not be rushed into this. Now, privately he can make it perfectly clear to the businessmen that he is pro-nuke and we can send all sorts of signals to that effect.

"But to really make it clear to these guys, we'll just go ahead with the reprocessing plant at Barnwell and get on with filling the salt caverns with waste material in New Mexico."

The President brooded, picking at the label on his new jeans. He glanced at Ham inquiringly.

"Fair enough Jody, but we've got to be tougher than that."

There was silence, broken only by the chink of Bert's gold bracelet he as raised the can and took another refreshing swallow of Tab.

"Well," Caddell broke in, "there is a game plan I sketched out on the way up here. The first part of it is remarkably similar to what Jody just said. But there are some other aspects. The first and most obvious thing to do is to get the FBI to increase surveillance of the demonstrators. Then we've got to start pumping money into local citizen groups that support us. I've advised my clients a lot about this sort of grass roots business organizing and I'll tell you there's just nothing like a local citizens group to give you value for walk around money.

"We could provide this funding through LEAA, or

better yet through that ACTION community crime control program."

"Say that's a great idea," Jordan broke in. "I'll bet Sam Brown is against nuclear power himself. No one would ever think that ACTION would be working for nuclear power."

The President brightened. "Sam Brown was a fine appointment. I've great confidence in him."

Caddell broke through the President's measured self-praise.

"Though Bert's grand jury idea wouldn't work, there is another way. There's nothing to stop us from establishing a special task force within the Justice Department to deal with intruders and sabotage at nuclear power plants and on energy supply lines. Why, we could even get some hearings fixed up on the Hill about national security and the internal sabotage threat—along the lines of that memorandum Jim Schlesinger gave Jimmy six months ago."

The President pondered once more. "To sum it up then, if I understand you right, we will indicate to the business community our support for nuclear power. Simultaneously I will reassure opponents of nuclear power that I am personally agonized by the dangers of nuclear power and have not yet come to a determination, and meanwhile we will press ahead with interdiction and prosecution of all activists in this field.

"Have I got it right?" He looked round the room hopefully. They nodded, Bert toasting Jimmy's accurate report with a genial wave of his Tab.

"One thing," said the President plaintively. "I'm not

going to have to do exactly the opposite of this plan next week, am I?"

"No, no, Jimmy. This is okay for the time being."

"Good. Now I must attend religious service with Rosalynn." He gave them all a kindly wave and strolled from the room, as Bert launched into a robust description of his latest adventures in the New Hebrides.

Equal Opportunity

The two women were embracing naked on the bed, lip to lip, thigh to thigh. They arched like salmon forging their way upstream for spring spawning. Prudence and Maria, their twined bodies an advertisement for equal opportunity.

Prudence was the serious one—all work and no play; no play, that is, until she met Maria. Prudence was an economics professor at the University of Pennsylvania, the Wharton School to be precise. Her specialty was administrative reorganization. On the recommendation of Professor Arthur Buskin she had been referred to the White House in the hot days of the Carter transition, where her name had caught the attention of the reorganization chief, Harrison Welford.

Welford had spoken to Prudence directly. "I am asking you to undertake what may probably be the most important professional act of your career. I am asking you to join with me in reorganizing the government of this country."

The next thing Prudence remembered was standing next to the President, one hand on the Bible and the other in the air, while swearing to uphold the laws of the United States. As she stood there, looking out on the beautiful spring day, flowers resplendent in the gardens around the White House, she allowed herself to steal a glance at her future employer: noble in bulk, tremendous in aspect—Bertram Lance.

Those had been glorious days in the lusty infancy of the administration. There had been trips to Paris to study French modes in budget decision-making and rationalization; exciting discussion of Rueff's gold theories with Suzette Longchamps, from the French Financial Ministry. Suzette's Gallic disdain for what she called "la budget zero-basée" had been delicious.

There had been the swift rushes to Capitol Hill, to confer with the poor ailing Humphrey (national interest always at heart); she had enjoyed the bluff Irish humor and courtly graces of Tip O'Neill; and suffered the impenetrable stupidity of Robert Byrd. Above all, there had been the infectious gaiety and indefatigable activity of Bert himself. He was inexhaustible in his efforts to bring business and government closer together. His office became a veritable traffic jam of American corporate adventure: oil men rubbed shoulders with bank lobbyists. In the throng in his outer

Equal Opportunity

office the swarthy features of Middle Eastern traders would contrast with the pallid hesitancy of milquetoast bureaucrats, attempting to deflect Bert's impetuous ways with red tape.

It had been amid the ghastliness of Bert's fall that, numbly pursuing her latest assignment and Bert's pet scheme—how to abolish the Federal Trade Commission—she had met Maria.

Maria's past was obscure. Seemingly Bolivian, possibly Honduran, for all Prudence knew, maybe Cuban, Maria was in the eyes of the law an illegal alien. Leaking Bert's plans to a *New York Times* newspaper reporter over a fine dinner at his house, Prudence had noticed Maria, the underpaid and discontented housekeeper.

Maria was swiftly engaged by Prudence to take charge of her Capitol Hill apartment. She was a great success. Her *porce con frijoles* became famed among the young Carter appointees invited by Prudence for long evenings of discussion and good times. There were the lions: Sam Brown, his keen mind ever probing for fresh ideas to help the poor—an urban fishpond here, a neighborhood garden there; Joan Claybrook, a brilliant woman and a brilliant politician; Eula Bingham, from the Occupational Safety and Health Administration. She had been too long in Cincinnati, Prudence thought to herself. She had never cared for Midge Costanza and was intimidated by Anne Wechsler, so adroit in sniffing the changing political climate from week to week in Carter's Washington. And there were the speech writers—a plaintive, overpaid lot, Prudence secretly considered—as they bemoaned the President's lack of interest in any rhetorical flourishes beyond the simple linkage of noun to verb and then to object.

It was one evening when she was helping Maria clear away a spectacular pork roast, much applauded by some non-smoking young Turks from HEW that, in companionably washing the dishes, she had felt Maria's thigh pressed against hers. The talk became slower. Dishes slipped from nerveless hands. And for Prudence the world turned upside down as Maria's tongue, in a leisurely way, searched and found and won her.

Summer passed, fall waned, and winter came amid their love. Bert fell. Harrison stayed. The Federal Trade Commission lived on. And Prudence gained an acceptance and popularity among the President's most intimate staff. There was scarcely a day when she did not see the men most closely associated with Jimmy Carter.

It was in the spring of 1979 that she first met an attractive young public interest lawyer called Julie Lindner. Julie had come to Washington to represent the New Jersey anti-nuclear groups in arguing against the reorganizing of the Federal Energy Department, a process that would have further denied local citizens' groups a right to intervene in nuclear power plant licensing.

Julie's vigorous style and sharp manner attracted Prudence and the two became close friends. For Julie a visit to Washington was, usually, a dinner with Prudence. Dinners with Prudence often became hot arguments about the President's energy policies and, struggle as she might, Prudence found herself hard put to defend the policies of the Administration.

One day, at the turn of the year, Prudence had been talking to Ham Jordan when her eye caught a thick file of papers on his desk, labelled TOP SECRET.

Prudence noted the topic, "Fuel Systems Supply," and when Jordan got up to run down the corridor and berate the Vice President for a poor performance before the American Medical Association she snitched the file and returned to her office. She copied it over the lunch hour and later dropped the original back in Jordan's office.

Prudence had no physical designs on Julie, but liked to please her nonetheless. The next time Julie came to Washington, Prudence, amid many injunctions to secrecy, off-handedly presented her with the file.

Looking back on it later, Prudence was never quite certain whether a jealous Maria had gone to the FBI or whether the FBI had somehow started to investigate Julie and tracked back to her.

What she did know was that two weeks after the incidents in Wilmington and Los Angeles, an FBI agent called and made a request to see her. She met him in the bar of the Mayflower Hotel and spent an hour in the front seat of his car, parked just outside.

He was very polite and made no overt threats. But it was clear that he knew she had given the papers to Julie. It was equally clear that the details of her personal life with Maria were known to him. Maria herself, he explained, could be expelled as an undocumented worker and Prudence charged with furnishing information likely to be of use to a foreign power. He dwelt casually on the Humphrey-Truong case. Then he indicated to a terrified Prudence that nothing "overly unpleasant" need happen.

The government, he said, wanted to find out more about the anti-nuclear movement and particularly the groups associated with Julie. She might be of great service.

Prudence thought about it overnight, and the next morning called the FBI. She agreed to future meetings with Special Agent Forsyth. She entertained with less zest than before.

The Big Time

"I for one will not tolerate the misuse of the democratic process by a small group of big shot crooks!"

The President, lying back in a hammock in his summer retreat on St. Simons Island, seemed to be addressing the American people on network television. There was silence except for the late July hum of insects and the distant raucous shouts of the Secret Service playing softball with the Carter public relations team.

He twisted his head round, and eyed his actual audience in the shape of just one man, William Miller, chairman of the Federal Reserve Board.

Miller allowed a brief silence and then laughed lightly.

"We're all against crooks, Jimmy. But of course all bankers aren't crooks."

"No, no, of course not. I was just thinking out loud." The President paused. Then he swung his feet down on the floor and began to speak seriously to a spot on the ground between his canvas loafers.

"Well look, Bill. I don't know what to do about this situation. You say the American banking community is in a state of crisis. But you're always saying it's in a state of crisis, and if you don't then one of the bankers will. Wriston, Rockefeller, Patterson: Christ, I don't know how many times I've come into the office in the morning to find one of them on the phone, bleeding on about some special deal. Tax credits for their oil in the North Sea. Troops to Zaire to help them save their assets there. Natural Gas in Thailand."

"Mr. President, this is different."

"Why?"

Miller began to talk rapidly.

"It's a simple fact that American banks have immense investments in the nuclear industry. And I'm not speaking solely about portfolios of utility stocks and bonds. Historically the big New York banks have stood solidly behind the electrical manufacturers, Westinghouse and General Electric. Those two companies are in a terrible state. Orders for the nuclear plants that they make are almost nonexistent. The West Germans and the French are stealing the business all over the world. Bankruptcy for electrical companies is not inconceivable."

The President looked up quickly. "You know I'm

pledged against another bailout. I can't have another Lockheed in an election year! Can you imagine what Proxmire would do with that?"

"That's precisely why I'm here," Miller said urgently. "Now, at the Fed we've been talking to some of the major bankers and with our sources abroad and we think we've got a solution. To put it simply, the Russians are very much committed to nuclear power, both for themselves and those within their sphere of influence. What the New York banking community wants to do is to take the pressures off the electrical manufacturers by selling nuclear power plant parts to the Soviets."

"To the Soviets?" The President reddened angrily. "To the Soviets! Can you imagine what Jackson and Moynihan would do with that, let alone the Republicans? You remember what I had to do after the Shcharansky trial? The bankers are out of their minds."

Miller raised his hand soothingly. "No, of course, not *directly* to the Russians. But these companies have subsidiaries in Asia, the Philippines, South Korea. We would propose simply to sell parts from the far eastern subsidiaries to the Japanese. The Japanese recently concluded a large-scale barter agreement with the Soviet Union, under which the Soviets agreed to supply oil and gas to the Japanese who need the fuels, in exchange for various high technology. Included in the category of high technology is nuclear power plant equipment."

The President continued to look puzzled. "But why in the name of God would the Japanese want to aid us like that?"

"Mr. President, this is a form of trading, which we've

already been conducting for some time. Some American nuclear equipment has been going to the Soviets to help them out in tight spots. The Russians have been providing the Cubans with nuclear power plant equipment, and when, some time ago, there was a shortage of parts we've met the shortfall."

Carter shook his head foggily. "But where do the Japanese come into this?"

"Well, the Japanese just act as middle-men and reconsign the equipment off their docks. It helps them in their relations with the Soviets. And we merely announce that it's the Japanese who are buying the stuff."

Suddenly it all dawned on the President and he sprang up and paced about the porch. "I see, I see. And of course there may be some other benefits! I'll bet Harold Brown would love the idea that those third world countries in the Soviet sphere would actually be dependent on our nuclear power plant equipment. What a magnificent idea! Just wait till the West Germans and the French hear about this one."

Carter sat down again, and then eyed Miller speculatively.

"Bill, you and the bankers are presumably asking the President of the United States to sanction such a major deal?"

Miller nodded.

The President examined his fingernails. "Of course you've got some personal interest in this, haven't you?"

Miller reddened and said abruptly, "All my holdings are in a blind trust."

"I know, I know," Carter said soothingly. "All our

holdings are in blind trusts. But I do recollect from FBI reports at the time of your confirmation hearings that you played a major part in purchasing for your old company Textron a big block of stock in Allied Chemical. And as we all know, Allied Chemical is very much involved in the the nuclear business. Presumably your trustee, at the very least, would be heartened if the nuclear business started to look up."

Miller waited, without saying anything.

There was a silence and in it they heard a distant roar from the softball game as Jody Powell struck out.

The President now seemed to change his tack. "Bill, I know that inflation is on your mind, as it is on mine."

"It's the number one problem in this country," Miller said automatically.

"Now one of the reasons," the President said thoughtfully, "that I decided not to reappoint Arthur Burns as chairman of the Fed was that he kept pushing interest rates up. High interest rates are not much of help to a politician like myself in an election year."

"No, Sir," Miller said, without thinking.

Carter stared directly at Miller. "But Bill, you've been pushing interest rates up all year."

Miller looked at the President strangely and then began to speak very formally, as though for the record.

"Mr. President, the decisions affecting interest rates are made by a committee of the Federal Reserve, of which I am only one. It is, of course, traditional that the chairman exercises some modicum of extra authority in these deliberations. I need not point out to you that of the twelve members no less than eight have essentially come out for higher interest rates at least to the end of this year. They represent the banking community, which is naturally concerned at the present business atmosphere."

Carter broke in quickly. "But from what you say, Bill, they are also concerned about the future of the nuclear industry and hence of these sales to the Soviet Union." He allowed his voice to die away and continued to eye Miller closely.

Miller said nothing. The President pressed forward. "Perhaps, given all these factors, some compromise might be reached?"

Miller looked around the porch and continued to speak formally.

"The Federal Reserve is an independent body—"

"I know," interrupted the President. "That's exactly what Arthur Burns said in 1972 when interest rates fell sharply, just in convenient time to help Richard Nixon win one of the largest reelection margins in American history."

Convention

The sun rose up that early August morning over Puget Sound, over Seattle, over that most glorious of all political enterprises: the Democratic Convention. It was a time for politics, a time for drinking, a time for screwing, a time of hope, and a time of hangover.

In the smoke-filled breakfast room of the Hilton two delegates from Maine were picking up useful information from a voluble Georgia state senator.

"What we Georgians like is to go turtle-hunting in the swamps and get us one of those snapping turtles, the size of an Eisenhower dollar. Then you get yourself one of them little turtles and you hang 'em on your cock."

"What do you do then?"
"You run around the halls of the state legislature."
"With the turtle on your cock?"
"Yessirree."

In the Holiday Inn, Senator Henry Jackson rehearsed his keynote speech in front of the mirror and the admiring eyes of Richard Perle, his trusted adviser on the cold war.

"In 24 hours the Soviet Union could be on the outskirts of Paris." Jackson's arm shot forward in an awkward rendition of the Nazi salute. "In 48 hours Britain would be overwhelmed." His arm dropped. "So I say we can strike first! We should strike first! We must strike first!"

Perle, his mind actually on the patent problems for the mass production soufflé-making machines he had invented, applauded.

In the Hyatt Inn, Fritz Mondale whimpered softly in his sleep. He was addressing the delegates. His mouth was full of sand. He looked up and there was the President looking down on him, weeping. The tears rose above his waist, above his eyes. Mondale screamed and awoke abruptly from the nightmare.

In the Ramada Inn, Richard Goodwin was on his fifth draft of a speech for Teddy Kennedy. "My fellow Americans, this is a time of fear, but a time for greatness. A time for leadership. We must not hope to fail, nor must we fail to hope." Goodwin tore the paper from the typewriter and threw it into the wastepaper basket.

In the Best Chance Motel two Texan delegates were bargaining with a guest, who had flown in from Minneapolis.

"Let me get this straight," said Lulubelle. "You boys want me to tie you up and read you the Bible?"

"Three sheet bends, a clove hitch, a bowline, and the Sermon on the Mount."

"That'll be a hundred dollars apiece, and for another hundred I'll hang you by your feet."

"Good deal."

Yes, it was the convention. All across town people braced themselves for the awesome responsibilities of nominating the next President (God willing) of the United States.

Out in the Sound a tug and barge lay at anchor, rolling slightly in the gentle swell. The barge was low in the water, with its cargo of nuclear fuel assemblies carefully stowed beneath lead shields. Until 5:30 that morning the tug and and barge had been bound for a military facility at the eastern end of the Sound. At about that time Captain Mark Stephens had observed two fifteen-foot fishing boats heading out past him. Stephens had paid them little heed and had retired to the head to shave.

At 6:05, as he later reported to a Board of Inquiry, he was ready to leave the head and tried to open the door. It wouldn't budge. He gave it a kick and realized that it was locked from the outside. He shouted. No answer came.

Captain Stephens then realized the tug was losing way and seconds later came the unmistakable sound of the anchor chain rattling overboard.

Herb Partridge was having his cup of coffee on the barge and reading a back issue of *Hustler.* He looked up as a shadow flitted across the porthole and found himself staring into the twin barrels of a twelve-gauge shotgun. Behind the shotgun he could observe a rounded bosom and above it a ski mask.

"Take off your clothes," croaked the ski mask.

Modestly embarrassed by *Hustler*-induced tumidity Partridge obliged.

"Lie on the deck, you sexist pig."

Partridge did as he was told.

By 6:20 that morning all crew members of the tug and barge were naked, lying face down.

Ten minutes later the boarding party lowered the tug's lifeboat, ordered the naked mariners on to it, thoughtfully equipped them with two oars and cast them adrift.

Up the mast of the tug, to the cheers of the assembled invaders, went something resembling the Japanese flag: red sun on white background—the banner of the Solar Alliance. The first stage of the operation had been successfully completed.

In the dingy Railway Inn, Jerry Brown was reading the newspapers. He noted with some satisfaction that his impromptu airport arrival speech with its digs at

Convention

Carter had received ample coverage from national correspondents, eager to brew up an epic convention drama.

The phone in the small suite rang and his chief aide Gray Davis picked it up.

"Yes, yes . . . What? . . . They want to talk to Brown? . . . Why?"

Davis listened some more. "Hold on."

Covering the receiver, he looked at Brown. "Jerry, it's the Coast Guard. There're some no-nuke people who've taken over a barge in the harbor. They want to talk to you, the Coast Guard says."

Brown thought for a moment, then shrugged his shoulders. "What will be will be."

He took the phone.

Out in the harbor Teresa O'Rourke took off her ski mask and began to shout into the radiotelephone, in declamatory fashion.

"Jerry, here's what's going down. The Solar Alliance has temporarily seized a barge carrying fuel rods. We want to symbolize the nation's opposition to nuclear power. We regard you as the only halfway sane person at this convention. You're the only person who can persuade the Democratic Party that No Nukes is the only policy."

Brown began cautiously. "Have . . . ah . . . any people been injured in this seizure?"

"No."

"What exactly is the Solar Alliance again?"

"The Solar Alliance is an organization which has pledged itself to action both direct and indirect, to delay, and then to cancel nuclear power in the United States. We are opposed to the proliferation of nuclear power in all forms, civil and military. Today we intend to compel the Democratic Convention to confront this issue. We want to force all the major politicians to make a commitment."

Brown thought ahead. "Well, you know, in my governorship California led the way in developing alternative sources of energy. Have you spoken to anyone else this morning?"

"Jerry, come on, you're the first. We're with you. Are you prepared to make a statement supporting the occupation?"

Brown thought some more. "What are you going to do with that barge?"

"If the Democratic Party supports a no-nukes policy the barge will be returned to its owners. If not—"

At this point a voice brusquely broke in on the line. "Governor, this is Commander O'Brien of the U.S. Coast Guard. You should know that this seizure of the barge is a violation of the law, and we have duly notified the proper authorities. All conversations between the hijackers and persons on shore are being monitored by the U.S. Coast Guard, the Federal Bureau of Investigation, and the Defense Department."

"Thank you for the information, Commander." Brown handed the telephone nervously back to Davis and started to calculate.

In Washington it was mid-morning when the telephone rang in the home study of the Secretary of Energy. After listening to the report of the Coast Guard, Schlesinger immediately placed a call first to the Governor of the State of Washington and then to the Pentagon.

All parties were in full agreement. The occupation had to be terminated at once, by force if necessary.

Plans moved swiftly. By 11 A.M. Pacific time, a special Ranger force was launching a mini-submarine, equipped with torpedoes and automatic weapons. Placed aboard were ten specially-trained commandoes assigned to the maritime interdiction detail. A Coast Guard launch was ordered to monitor the assault from the surface. As the sub sank from view into the murky waters of Puget Sound, Governor Dixie Lee Ray was ordering the first of ten contingents of National Guardsmen to patrol the shores of the Sound.

Hamilton Jordan first became aware of the occupation when he picked it up from a local all-news radio station. He placed a call to the Coast Guard, only to be informed that efforts to recover the vessel were underway, but that plans to this end could not be discussed on an insecure line. Minutes passed before he made contact with the Secretary of Energy, who briskly outlined the strategy.

Jordan exploded in rage. "Mr. Secretary, do you realize that in this recovery mission people are bound to be seriously hurt. The President himself is about to land in Seattle. If you have your way, he'll have to face Convention delegates, not to mention the world's press, aware that this administration has probably provoked the greatest loss of life in an internal incident since Kent State. Do you want to spend the rest of this campaign testifying in front of a board of inquiry? Do you want to spend a few years in a minimum security prison?"

Schlesinger's voice returned pompously. "The operation is now underway. It cannot be stopped."

Jordan, sweating heavily, placed a call to Air Force One, at that point in a holding pattern over Seattle, awaiting Secret Service clearance to land.

"Jimmy," began Jordan.

"Hi, Ham."

"We've got trouble, Jimmy. Some anti-nuclear demonstrators have seized a barge in the harbor here. It's loaded with some kind of nuclear junk, and that goddam nut Schlesinger has sent in the commandoes. They're due to board any time now. Someone may very well be killed."

"Oh shit. What do we do now?"

"Well, Jimmy, you could fire Schlesinger, but it probably would not make much difference."

"But can't we stop this," Carter said plaintively, trying to peer down to the Sound fifteen thousand feet below. "I'm the Commander in the Chief after all. Can't I be placed in communication with the demonstrators?"

Three minutes later the President was in simultaneous conversation with James Schlesinger and Teresa O'Rourke.

"Miss O'Rourke, this is your Commander in Chief. I

Convention

have told the Secretary of Energy that . . . ah . . . if you and your colleagues immediately put down your weapons, lower your flag, and lie face down on the barge, severe measures presently being contemplated will be ah . . . deferred.

"You hear that, Jim," Carter barked into the other phone.

Three fathoms below the barge Ranger Lieutenant Hodgetts trained his torpedo tube at the target and stroked the firing button anxiously. On the surface the Coast Guard launch was racing at full speed across the Sound, with a cargo of commandoes ready to board.

Teresa began hectoring the President. Would he make a speech opposing nuclear power? Would he announce an immediate moratorium on all nuclear projects? Would he—

"Anything. I'll say anything you want me to," shrieked the President, trying to deflect Schlesinger from the immediate resignation being threatened on the other telephone.

Their voices rose in a crescendo of threats and pleadings as Lieutenant Hodgetts suddenly received an order to surface and monitor the surrender of the barge. Trained to obey, Hodgetts excitedly shot the mini-sub upwards. As he broke surface he looked out the starboard porthole, just in time to see the magnificent bow wave of the Coast Guard launch bearing down on him at full speed.

Smoke

At the helm of the launch, Officer Thorkstein gave a little cry as he spun the wheel hard to port. His hope, he subsequently explained at the court-martial proceedings, had been to avoid a collision with the mini-sub by passing between it and the barge.

It was too late. There was a grinding crash as the launch bows sheared the stern off the mini-sub before slamming sideways into the barge.

All three craft began to sink as the President continued to argue with his Secretary of Energy. On the shore, Jerry Brown, with an eye cocked over his shoulder at the barge now clearly sinking with its Solar Flag still aloft, began a cautious press conference.

Life After Death

Teresa O'Rourke looked beautiful and at peace, as she lay resplendent in her $5,000 titanium casket in the Savage Funeral Home. Her grieving parents, fresh in from Cleveland, stood with stunned and mournful aspect, receiving Teresa's friends. Every so often they would steal a glance through the porthole of the casket at their daughter's face, tranquil—it seemed to them—for the first time in her life of anger: at the invasion of Cambodia, the treatment of the poor, the outrages against minorities, saccharin, abortion deaths, the invasion of southern Lebanon, paraquat, injustice to the handicapped, and, of course, nuclear power.

Mr. and Mrs. O'Rourke had, as they say, lost touch

Smoke

with their daughter in recent years. Occasionally a passing FBI man would bring news of the latest charges pressed against her in various parts of the country. In her more vehement moments of protest against the nuclear family, Teresa herself would dispatch them prolonged letters of abuse. It was hard sometimes to figure if she had sent them, since they were signed under various symbolic pseudonyms. There had the puzzling card from Alexandra Kollontai, sent from Berkeley; the abusive tirade, with death threats, from Lily; the distasteful pornographic self-portrait, with an accompanying note announcing entry into the trade of prostitution from "Sappho." There were other clues to Teresa's whereabouts. The trail of charge account bills on Mr. O'Rourke's family American Express card. The FBI put a stop to that and Teresa vanished further and further into the underground.

Her body had been washed up three miles down the Sound the day after the barge occupation and subsequent unfortunate collision. Mr. O'Rourke, reasonably distraught, listened to the snatches of conversation going around him. A small bespectacled man wearing a No-Nuke badge attempted to relieve Mrs. O'Rourke in her anguish: ". . . forty extra quads of energy by the year 2000. And with cogeneration, not to mention district heating and proper harnessing of biomass there is no reason the soft path could be taken."

Mr. O'Rourke lost the thread, for a man whom he thought had identified himself as "Bill Jarndyce, Movement Lawyer" was jerking at his elbow. "Just flew in from Lame Deer. Soon as I heard the news. A wonderful, beautiful, tragic girl. I knew her well. A beautiful person."

"She was, she was," Mr. O'Rourke sighed.

Jarndyce pressed forward. "You mustn't let it go, Mr. O'Rourke. It's too important. The information on discovery will be very helpful to the movement. Her death is a real opportunity to move forward. We hope to announce the Teresa O'Rourke Committee today."

"Committee?"

"Right."

"What for?"

"For Teresa. Don't you see the opportunity? Let's take the case up to the Supreme Court. They hounded her. We'll hound them. Remember the Chicago Seven."

"Seven?"

"And the Catonsville Nine."

"Nine?"

"Joan Little. The Boston Twelve. Karen Silkwood." Jarndyce lowered his voice.

"I'm suggesting to you, Mr. O'Rourke, that you hold a press conference over your daughter's open grave. Announce that you do not intend to let this matter drop. That you are going to sue the government. That you are pledging your wealth to the formation of a Defense Committee."

Mr. O'Rourke, alerted at last by the mention of money, broke in.

"Defense campaign? But she's dead. What will we be defending?"

Jarndyce scarcely broke stride.

Smoke

"The right of people to protest the government's nuclear conspiracy, which reaches to every man, woman and child in this country. The government is slowly poisoning the people." His voice rose. "What are the people meant to do? Die? Lodge an environmental impact statement? Did the people of Hiroshima lodge an impact statement?"

By now Jarndyce was thundering to the entire funeral parlor and sporadic cheers were breaking out.

"Let me tell you, people, Mr. O'Rourke has just told me that he is opening a campaign to seek justice for the murder of Teresa." Roars of applause. Mr. O'Rourke looked blank and then a smile crept across his forlorn face as Jarndyce raised the bereaved man's arm, and held it high, tactfully molding Mr. O'Rourke's fingers into a fist.

Mr. O'Rourke stared at the fist for a few seconds, then shook it tentatively. Jarndyce released his grip. Mr. O'Rourke began to waggle his fist with increasing fervor as cheers swelled around him, rolling across his dear, lost Teresa's casket in thunderous billows, out into the street. To Mr. O'Rourke's suddenly ecstatic ears it seemed as though the cheers were bursting into the convention center itself, into the booth of Walter Cronkite, into the transmitters, and out across the length and breadth of America.

He bent for a moment to Jarndyce. "How much money do you think we need?"

Jarndyce had done his organizing well. The graveyard was packed, filled with television, newspaper, and

Life After Death

magazine reporters, glad to take an hour off from the monotony of an Adoption of Platform debate at the Convention Hall. "Good media," he told Mr. O'Rourke cryptically, as they and four other pallbearers struggled under the weight of the titanium casket.

"My God this is heavy," Mr. O'Rourke heard Tom Hayden grunt from the rear. Slowly they tottered forward, until finally Mr. O'Rourke could see the maw of the open grave itself ahead with a pile of moist soil well trodden by photgraphers alongside. His heart gave a sudden lurch. For from the grave itself a head seemed slowly to be emerging. And a head indeed it was, on the shoulders of a photographer from the *New York Post* who had been ensconced there waiting for a dramatic shot.

The coffin was finally lowered and Jarndyce and O'Rourke prepared to address a a glorious host of mourners including Ramsay Clark, George McGovern, Gene McCarthy, and Hongisto of New York.

O'Rourke was by now a zealous convert to direct action against what he was casually referring to as "the Rockefeller Conspiracy that Murdered My Daughter." Under Jarndyce's approving gaze he opened a lengthy oration written by Jarndyce the day before. He cleared his throat, only to find that he was losing his audience before he had even begun.

Heads were turning toward the back of a crowd, from whence came a murmur. There was jostling, and cries of recognition. A space opened and a slim lone figure with dark hair and a formal suit strode in a businesslike manner toward the grave-site. O'Rourke found himself shoved aside by a swarm of photographers; he lost his footing and tumbled into the grave itself. Holding a sprained ankle he could hear a disembodied voice, peered up, and recognized the profile of Jerry Brown.

"Ad altaria dei introibamus."

A look of bewilderment spread across Mr. O'Rourke's countenance. Brown, raising his hand to quell the crowd, continued.

"Filia coeli beatissima est. Ex ossibus oriat ultor. Let us pray for this dear child."

Mr. O'Rourke struggled to get out of the grave. The governor cleared his throat. "Teresa's outwardness is now inward. Things must pass but they must also return. Things come and things go. Amen."

There was a surge of reporters.

"Governor, what are your plans now you have failed to gain the nomination?"

"I will swim among the people like a fish in the sea."

"Will you support the President?"

"Does the President need my support?"

"Will you work for the Party?"

"I will work for a party that I can work with."

"Does that mean you are bolting the Democratic Party?"

"I shall move among the people."

Brown turned and made his way out of the crowd, perched himself on the back of Jacques Barzhagi's motorcycle, and roared off down the road, with a friendly wave.

Back in Cleveland Mr. and Mrs. O'Rourke used often to peer at the front pages of the national press which they kept as a memento of their exciting trip. Down in the left hand corner there were brief reports of Teresa's death and interment. The main headlines roared out the simple message, "BROWN BOLTS PARTY."

CREAK

All during the fall, the Carter Re-election Campaign, nicknamed CREAK by the wags, sustained blow after blow.

The interest rate scandal broke in September in the pages of the *Wall Street Journal;* the 1976 campaign fund scandal shortly thereafter. The anti-nuclear campaign did not go away. The bid to liberate U.S. technicians kidnapped in French Equatorial Guinea ended in fiasco with the most powerful country on earth a supplicant to what Senator Moynihan called "a barbarian savage."

The Republicans picked up support from the well-oiled business lobby. Robert Strauss changed parties. And then with the force of a tornado, the zirconium scandal broke over the beleaguered White House.

It was a typical Washington story, shone to a high gloss by William Safire.

There was General Anwat; Saudi Arabian by birth, educated at West Point and subsequently distinguished in his work for the Central Intelligence Agency. He was a brilliant economist, well known among his colleagues at Langley for his shrewd business deals. It had been no secret for years that certain high rollers in the CIA's photo-reconnaissance division had been making a bundle by using satellite-acquired foreknowledge of Soviet crop conditions to play the futures market in the United States. General Anwat honed this art to perfection.

It was he who had engineered the famous Franco-Belgian cobalt play in Zaire in 1978. By persuading both the French and the Belgians that each would profit from closure of the Shaba mines he had driven up the black market price of cobalt and subsequently reaped the great benefits of having bought the commodity dirt cheap some months before the invasion.

After his CIA duty in Langley, Anwat had returned to his native land where he helped develop the Saudi intelligence service and, because of his renowned successes in finance, played a growing role in the investment of the Royal Family's fortunes. Of great use to him in his various investment decisions were some in the Georgian banking community and the soft drink company, whose removal from the Arab blacklist he had intrigued for as early as 1975.

Since his earliest days in the CIA, Anwat had been a

close associate of one Harry Larsen. Larsen was a spe-
cialist in photo interpretation for the CIA and in their
halcyon days together they had enjoyed cruises in the
Aegean, drifting pleasantly from island to island. By
1978, Larsen found himself hard-pressed financially. He
needed alimony, money to put his children through
school, and even more money for a hip operation.

In the Turner purges of 1977, he had received the
final blow of being forced out of the Agency itself and
given a lesser-paying job in one of the CIA's subcon-
tracting organizations in Rosslyn. It was here that he
rekindled his friendship with Anwat, while helping to
designate fishery sites in the Middle East, then thought
to be a shrewd investment.

One night, sitting comfortably in the Riyadh Hilton,
Larsen broached to Anwat the prospects for a financial
coup rivalling the great cobalt play itself. It involved a
little-known commodity called zirconium.

Larsen knew all about zirconium. In his CIA days he
had spent months studying the movements of this commodity, a sand mineral used in making heat-resistant
shielding for nuclear power plants and in the manufacture of other industrial products.

Zirconium, Larsen explained to Anwat, came in sub-
stantial quantities from Florida and Georgia, but was
most plentifully found in Australia.

Larsen had a plan.

Anwat would buy out the lone independent company dealing in zirconium in Florida and Georgia, outside the big conglomerates such as Dupont. Then, using
Anwat's ties to Georgian bankers and their intimate

relationships with the administration, they would secure a zirconium contract with a power plant manufac-
turer.

"But my dear Larsen," Anwat had said patronizingly,
"what about the Australian supplies? There's a big over-
hang in the market. Our zirconium would be more or
less worthless. We might as well try to corner petunia
seeds."

Larsen laughed. "I knew you were going to ask that.
I have a very simple solution."

His solution was not in fact simple, but seemed
nonetheless workable to Anwat. They would intrigue
through old CIA agents in place in the Australian labor
unions to foment a strike and sabotage zirconium shipments to the United States. Some Australian unions
were militantly opposed to nuclear power. It would not
take much effort to rouse their animosity. This would
then narrow the zirconium market at the precise moment when nuclear power plant production in the
United States was slated to increase; and, Larsen added,
at the precise moment when their independent zirconium company in Florida would make a public offering of stock.

On September 4, 1979, Z.I.R. Inc., an independent
zirconium-producing company in Florida, made a public offering. The stock opened at 10 and within three
days was selling at 25. In six months it was at 35. By
Labor Day, 1980 Z.I.R. Inc.'s stock was at 110 and it had
secured contracts with the major electrical manufacturers, was doing business with TVA and other government nuclear facilities, and had been hailed by business

weeklies as one of the most up and coming companies of the decade.

A week later, the bubble burst. The stock slumped to 2. There was an investigation by the SEC. The newspapers, treading carefully within the constraints on business reporting established by the Supreme Court, hinted at the existence of a zirconium ring involving administration insiders, the CIA, and the Saudi Royal Family. Liz Smith, Herb Caen, and Jack Anderson devoted columns to the affair all the way through September and the first part of October. General Anwat and Larsen, who had bailed out at the top of the market, sat the storm out on a yacht in the Aegean.

The SEC report satisfied no one. Nor did the hearings held by Senator Frank Church, who spent more time ingratiating himself with the Republican inquisitors than in asking pertinent questions.

The Georgian investors, sheltered behind street names in their holdings in Z.I.R., were never exposed. But the President's guarded references to the affair in in town meetings left questions unanswered and the taint of scandal unmistakably lingering around his administration. He continued to slip in the polls.

Playing to Win

They gathered in Hamilton Jordan's spacious second-floor corner office in the White House. Jordan, in view of the seriousness of the occasion, was wearing a shirt by L.L. Bean, loose cotton trousers gathered at the ankles with a red ribbon in the Zen tradition, and red Adidas running shoes trimmed with blue piping. Powell had on an unbuttoned vest above denim cutaways and a rakish bowler. A formal note was struck by Charles Kirbo and Attorney General Griffin Bell. The older men were in classic pinstripe, with fashionably narrowed lapels and roll-up collar. The only jarring note in the sartorial harmony was Bell's filthy handkerchief which he constantly pulled from his pocket to blow his nose. Caddell was in his traditional fustian.

Bell came straight to the point.

"Judge Webster has just sent me this memorandum, based on a most reliable source. Let me tell you what it says quickly. Webster's people predict on the basis of certain information that an extremist anti-nuclear group is on the verge of plotting and carrying out a takeover of a big power plant. Webster's men suspect that this power plant will be somewhere in New Jersey —maybe around Salem."

"Salem," Jordan butted in. "Where's that?"

"I had to look it up myself. Salem is a nuclear complex, below the Delaware Memorial bridge, which itself is down from Wilmington and Philadelphia. It's off by itself. There's a little town, a lot of farmland."

"Okay Judge. Tell us what's planned," said Powell.

"The source who has penetrated this group says that the demonstrators are thinking of striking right before the election and shutting down the plant. This shut down could mean blackouts from Washington to Boston."

There was a silence.

"Well now Griffin," Charles Kirbo, Carter's most trusted outside adviser, broke in. "You know these FBI reports. How do we know this isn't a group of kooks feeding the Bureau a line, or talking big after drinking too much?"

"That's exactly what I asked Webster. Let me tell you what he said. Webster takes this seriously. He's got files as thick as a telephone book. He's got recorded telephone conversations, conversations between people standing on street corners."

"He's probably got people screwing too," said Jordan laconically.

"He has, as a matter of fact. I've read some of the transcripts."

"So what we have here," Caddell said thoughtfully, "is the probability of a piece of nuclear sabotage days before the election. The President would have to spend the last moments of the campaign attempting to negotiate—an open-ended test of his leadership."

"Exactly," said Bell excitedly. "We can't afford this."

"No, we can't," Kirbo echoed. "The polling data you brought in yesterday, Pat, was pretty grim. Brown and the other third-party types are really cutting into our base. We've been trying to surface the stuff about Baker and his coal mines, but nobody seems to care. Did you read Evans & Novak this morning? And Ham, the Jews are really screwing you for those cracks about the Israeli lobby you've been making over the years."

"I know, I know," groaned Jordan, taking a large pinch of snuff to relieve his anguish.

Bell glanced down at his memo pad. "Here's what I recommend. That we move expeditiously to make preemptive arrests on the grounds of conspiracy to sabotage a power plant. We have a Pentagon report in the works which will show that the Salem plant is essential to national security. That'll strengthen our case."

Jordan looked unhappy. "The trouble is, Judge, that'd look like a last-minute stunt on our part. Can't you see what would happen. These weedy guys, talking about solar energy and organic shithouses, being accused of putting together a conspiracy against the United States, on the basis of illegally-gathered information. Some informant you probably can't produce or even identify. The liberals would kill us, Brown will slaughter us, and the Republicans will just make hay. And anyway, Judge, you said yourself that the FBI was not certain they were actually going to do this."

There was another long silence.

Pat Caddell straightened up in his chair. "There is," he said softly, "a way this could really help us. But I'm not sure I should even say what it is. Are we secure in this room, Ham?"

Jordan shrugged, "The last sweep we had showed up with three different bugs. I reckon two were left over from Haldeman. The other was kind of old, according to the Secret Service. They reckon Lyndon Johnson probably had it put in and everyone forgot about it."

"Alright," said Caddell taking a deep breath. "Here's what I think. We should let the occupation plan proceed. We should even encourage it. We should try to make sure, through the informant, that this occupation occurs exactly four days before the election and that it initially succeeds."

"In the name of God," burst in Bell. "This is madness. Jimmy will never stand for it."

Kirbo nodded agreement.

"Let me finish. Remember, we have no certain evidence as yet that the sabotage will occur. But once it has, you can be sure that the extremists will make demands. They will want to talk to the President himself. Think of this in terms of media. The first day there will

Playing to Win

be a tremendous crisis. The saboteurs will have the headlines. The ball will be in their court. Then, our response. First we'll announce negotiations and tell them that the Vice-President will be sent to talk to them. That will show we're reasonable. But before the Republicans accuse of us of appeasement we'll move."

"How?" Bell stuttered, blowing his nose loudly.

"Jimmy will go on national television on the evening of the second day of the occupation—two days before the election. He will make the greatest speech of his life. He will say that the nation's security is deeply jeopardized; that the country cannot be held to ransom. He can even imply that foreign terrorists are part of the occupation. He'll speak from the War Room in the White House basement. He will announce that even while he is speaking groups of Rangers have landed and are regaining control of the plant. We will hold the networks for at least an hour and a half in prime time. At the end of it Jimmy will anounce that the plant has been secured, the terrorists are in custody. Remember the *Mayaguez* was a peak for Ford in the polls. At one stroke Jimmy will have regained the initiative, and there will be no time for Brown or the Republicans to try to take it away."

"My God," said Kirbo softly. Bell blew his nose again. Jordan and Powell, after fresh pinches of snuff, looked at each other for a moment, then nodded.

"Pat is thinking along very interesting lines," said Jordan. "Well, gentlemen, are there any immediate objections to his plan?"

Smoke

Bell shrugged. "I guess John Mitchell has left a nice cell behind him in the federal penitentiary. I guess it would not mean more than two years in jail with time off for medical attention. Charlie?"

Kirbo looked at his fingernails. "Speaking just as a country lawer, Pat, I guess that's a pretty effective last-minute appeal to the jury."

"So we're all agreed." Caddell looked round the room.

"Judge Webster's really going to be pissed," said Bell. "He thought this would be his first big conspiracy case and he was kind of looking forward to it. And another thing, his appointment doesn't expire in January. He's there whoever wins the election. Maybe he'll want to put some interesting material in the way of the Republican National Committee. Have you thought of that?"

Jordan yawned. "Don't worry about Webster. He's okay. He'll think twice before doing anything stupid like that."

Bell rose to his feet glancing at his watch. "I've got to run. I've got to address the National Democratic Women's Club in fifteen minutes."

"What are you going to talk to them about?" Powell asked.

"Oh, that goddam Burger and equal access and all that shit."

"One thing before you go," Caddell said, "there's the matter of who does the on-the-spot negotiating with the terrorists before the Rangers go in."

They scratched their heads.

Playing to Win

As the men debated the door suddenly flew open and there was the Vice-President of the United States. He was finely attired in a Boy Scout uniform.

"Why in the name of God are you wearing that?" Powell asked Mondale.

Mondale gazed down sheepishly at his attire. "I've just come from the keynote speech at the jamboree and I haven't had time to change. I thought I'd look in because I heard in the mess you were having a meeting and I didn't want to be left out. Jimmy did say, you know, that I could go to any meeting I wanted. You remember that, don't you Jody?"

Powell nodded.

"And anyway," Mondale pressed on, "I wonder if any of you would like to play tennis with me? Jimmy said I could use his court for half an hour this afternoon, just as soon as his uncle's stepsister's boyfriend's gardener gets off."

They all stared at Mondale. "Fritz," said Jordan in a kindly way, "we were just having a private chat about old times in Georgia. Nothing for you to bother with."

"I love those Georgia political stories," Mondale said eagerly as he plumped himself down in a chair.

He looked around the room hopefully. Finally, Kirbo rose sighing, and said, "Okay Fritz, I'll play tennis with you. Let's go."

"Oh goody." Mondale frisked out the door with a merry whistle.

As they watched the door close behind Mondale, Caddell said slowly, "Dangerous though it might be, Jimmy does need someone to negotiate at the plant

Smoke

before the Rangers go in. It's a tough thing to order any man into an assignment like that."

Then they all laughed. "Fritz will do it," Powell said. "Especially if we don't tell him about the Rangers."

"Yes he will," said Caddell. "Fritz will do anything."

After the Sparrow Landed

Julie's mouth was dry and she watched Jack's hands tremble slightly as he shouldered his pack of food and clothing. Odd and random thoughts clustered in her mind: Teresa's funeral, the legal pleadings in Washington, and Prudence's puzzlingly strained air at their last meeting when she had said that after thinking about Julie's disclosure three weeks before that an occupation at Salem was being planned, in her opinion it was the only thing left to do. Militancy had never been Prudence's most visible asset in the past.

All that was behind them now.

It was just before dawn on a Saturday, November 1, 1980, four days before the election, when 32 people gathered outside the Salem nuclear complex, pushed aside the guards and entered the inner security area. Within fifteen minutes they had ejected the company officials and technicians and taken over the plant.

They were almost impregnable behind the thick doors of the nuclear station. Among the participants were nuclear scientists and energy experts. Every man and woman had been trained for weeks in the operations of a nuclear power plant. What made the Salem takeover different from all other efforts was that it involved some of the plant's own employees, themselves recruited into the anti-nuclear direct action ranks.

At 7 A.M. Julie placed a call to the White House and was quickly put on to Hamilton Jordan. She outlined their demands: The occupation would continue and the station gradually rendered inoperable unless certain conditions were fulfilled. The President must declare a moratorium on nuclear power construction. All government data on health and safety hazards in the nuclear industry must be made public at once. A special prosecutor must be appointed and given a free hand to investigate the activities of all government security agencies against the anti-nuclear movement.

Hamilton Jordan, she noticed, did not sound unduly concerned and assured her he would get back to her right away. Half an hour later he was back on the phone.

"The President has instructed the Vice-President to proceed as soon as is feasibly possible to discuss your demands with you. Our only request is that you not shut down the power until he arrives to make known the President's position."

It was not until early evening that Mondale, who had been campaigning in Illinois, was retrieved and briefed on his mission. Unknown to Mondale, at Bowling Air Force Base, red alert signals flashed in the Ranger ready room, and 300 elite commandoes, heavily armed, prepared to board the helicopters warming up on the tarmac.

As Mondale's chopper touched down on the Salem tarmac the Vice-President braced himself for the long ordeal ahead. He looked curiously about him. He had never seen a nuclear power plant before, despite Schlesinger's constant invitations to spend a picnic weekend with him and his family in the Clinch River breeder plant, now thankfully completed.

Inside, with only two aides permitted to accompany him, everything seemed normal enough and Mondale shook hands with the occupiers. He was mildly surprised at their trim appearance and quiet mien. Many were young and some were beautiful, and he found himself eyeing with some interest the curvaceous young woman at the plant controls. He tried to concentrate on the lecture he was now being given.

". . . So you see, Mr. Mondale," said a young, bearded electrical engineering professor from MIT, "the soft energy path versus the hard energy path will produce quite enough quads for U.S. consumption in the early 1980s. Not to mention total amortization of investment in solar, biomass, and ocean systems by the year 2025. And you'll be glad to know, Sir, that none of this—absolutely none of this—depends upon the space colony ideas of Jerry Brown."

Mondale winced at the mention of Brown.

"Did you know, Sir," Jack was saying, "that as long ago as 1977 the government itself had hard evidence that a competitive solar photovoltaic industry could begin at once. And that if 20 percent of the DOD's fuel-operated electric generator sets had been converted to photovoltaic systems, nearly half a billion dollars would have been saved by now?"

Mondale nodded feebly, thinking that the voice of the young man was slightly reminiscent of the manic drone of Energy Czar Schlesinger himself. Those endless lectures in the White House . . . Mondale found himself eyeing the trim ankles of the girl at the controls.

A day later Mondale never wanted to hear the words solar energy again. The zealous occupiers had crammed him with the history and perspectives of alternate energy. He knew about biomass, wave power, wind power, tidal power, energy conservation, heat pumps, sail power. Above all, he knew about solar power. And he knew very clearly what the occupiers wanted.

"It's like this, Mr. President," he reported wearily into the phone, "they want publication of all secret reports. They want the announcement of a moratorium. And they want you to cut the crap, as they put it, and do something serious about solar power. They want Schlesinger out now. I've tried to negotiate with them along the lines you suggested, but they're not willing to settle for a Camp David seminar. They think you're a liar. They want action now."

"They sound like a determined body of young men and women," said the President quietly. "I want to thank you, Fritz, for doing a great job. Tell them from me that we're working on the problem."

"But, Mr. President," Mondale faltered, "what do I do now?"

"Just hang in there, Fritz. Ham or Jody will be in touch."

While Mondale was on the phone the occupiers held their own huddled meeting in another room. As Mondale put down the phone and came back to the table Julie told him solemnly, "I'm sorry, Mr. Mondale, but since you are obviously not going to do anything we have begun to shut down power in the state of New Jersey. We are stopping the turbines, which means that electricity won't go out. And we fully expect that other utilities in this grid can't make up the difference and will have to begin load-shedding. I'm talking about New York and Boston. Do you want a blackout on election day, Mr. Vice-President?"

In the White House operations room they were running over the plans for the fourth time.

"Tell me, Jim," said the President, "is there the slightest danger that a nuclear accident can occur when

Smoke

the Rangers go in?" Schlesinger puffed powerfully on his pipe and then shook his head. "No chance at all."

Fritz Mondale's throat was dry as he watched Walter Cronkite announce that the President would start speaking in five minutes. *What was going on?* In their last conversation, Jody Powell had just told him to take it easy and to "keep talking." Then, just as the cameras focused on Carter in the War Room at the White House, he could hear the sound of distant firing, and the heavy thud of explosions against the safety doors.

The President was speaking now.

"The nation cannot be held to ransom—"

"You lied to us," Jack shouted at Mondale.

". . . New Jersey under martial law. Strike teams of specially-trained Rangers are now entering the plant . . ."

Mondale rose in panic.

". . . Order is now being restored . . ."

As he dashed toward the safety doors they burst open and a platoon of Rangers crashed into the room.

"Not me, not me," screeched Mondale. "Them, over there." He pointed at Jack and Julie, clutching each other in a corner.

His words were drowned in the thrum of machine gun fire. All fell quiet.

Meltdown

Two hours after the Salem Plant was recaptured, government technicians discovered that in the course of the attack the switchyard containing all the circuit breakers for the plant's electrical systems had been put out of action.

Champagne celebrations in the White House were interrupted by a phone call. It was for Schlesinger.

"What does this mean?" asked Schlesinger as he heard the technician in Salem report the damage.

"It means that the fuel rods in the reactor core have overheated beyond a point we can contain. It looks like it's too late to scram the system."

"Scram?" muttered Schlesinger. "What the hell does that mean?"

Smoke

"Well, Sir," said the technician with a tone of surprise, "it means an emergency shut down. But it's too late for that. The readings show that the temperature in the reactor core is now high enough for the fuel rods to melt. And that means, Sir, that we have almost certainly got a meltdown on our hands."

"Does that mean the reactor is going to be out of action?" snapped Schlesinger.

"Well, in a way, Sir, I suppose you could say that."

"That's okay, then," said Schlesinger with a sigh of relief.

"Not exactly, Sir. It means that we have a puddle of molten fuel collecting at the bottom of the reactor core. If we're not very lucky this could form a critical mass, with consequent release of energy and high radioactivity."

"You mean, an atom bomb?" Schlesinger's throat was dry, as Jody Powell tugged at his jacket to get him to rejoin the merriment.

"A sizable explosion would be a more accurate way of putting it. At the least, we could have a disastrous release of radioactivity. I suggest you implement total evacuation right away, for at least 40 miles downwind. And if the fuel is in the correct geometrical configuration, we could have something much worse. We could have—"

His words were suddenly cut off.

Five minutes later, Schlesinger brushed past Powell, his face ashen. He walked up to the President, who was putting down the telephone with a thoughtful air.

"Mr. President," said Schlesinger stiffly, "we've just lost New Jersey."

"That's nothing," said Jimmy. "You want to know what the Secretary of Defense just told me?"